ECHO

HOUNDS OF HELLFIRE MC

FIONA DAVENPORT

Copyright © 2025 by Fiona Davenport

Cover designed by Elle Christensen

Edited by Jenny Sims (Editing4Indies)

All rights reserved.

No part of this book may be reproduced in any form or by any electronic or mechanical means, including information storage and retrieval systems, without written permission from the author, except for the use of brief quotations in a book review.

❋ Created with Vellum

ECHO
HOUNDS OF HELLFIRE MC

Brodie "Echo" Fauks never expected to fall in love with a voice. Then he overheard Violet Kimball narrating a steamy scene in an audiobook while he was running surveillance on a conman who'd run afoul of the Hounds of Hellfire MC.

Violet's creepy neighbor was the road captain's target. When Echo discovered the guy had an interest in her, he came up with the perfect plan—pretend to be Violet's boyfriend. At least until she realized their relationship was very real.

1

ECHO

Surveillance could be boring as fuck, but I'd take tedium over the bullshit coming out of this asshole's mouth any day.

Jeff—the asshole in question—laughed, the sound grating on my ears.

"She's got a fat ass, but that just means more to hold on to when I fuck it."

Anger stirred in my chest, and I clenched my fists, talking myself out of storming over there and beating the shit out of him.

Apparently, Jeff had taken a liking to his neighbor. Every time he talked about her, his disgusting words and tone made me feel like I needed a shower.

I'd never seen her, but from what he said, it sounded like she was sweet and innocent. I hated to think what this motherfucker would do to her if given the opportunity.

Jeff was a con man. He swindled women out of every dime they had. Although, how the smarmy shit managed that, I had no clue.

One of his victims had come to the Hounds of Hellfire, the motorcycle club I belonged to. We were in the business of helping people "disappear" for a fee, although we made exceptions from time to time, especially if the victim was running from an abusive spouse or assholes who were worse than Jeff.

In this case, Tina didn't need to go on the run, but she'd come to us hoping we could recover her life savings and take down the scum who'd conned her.

Typically, we would have already dealt with him, but after listening to Tina's account a few times and doing some research, it didn't look like Jeff was calling the shots.

The president of my club, King, wanted to take down the whole operation, a decision we were all in agreement with.

Surveillance had been my specialty while serving in the Marines. I could pick up on things that others rarely heard, knew how to manipulate voices and noises to make them sound like anything we wanted to, and therefore, how to break them down to the original.

This was how I ended up in the apartment across the hall from Jeff's, listening to all of his conversations for a hint of the next link in the chain.

After a few days of being forced to listen to his shit, I'd started to worry more about the neighbor—Violet Kimball, according to her lease.

So last night, I rigged up some equipment to allow me to listen to the hallway and her apartment as well. I didn't put in cameras, tap her phone, or set up remote access to her electronics like I was working on for Jeff. But I wanted to make sure I would be alerted if he decided to pull any shit, and she needed rescuing.

Jeff hung up the phone—saving his life, for the moment—and from what I could hear afterward, it sounded as though he was getting ready to leave. Once he was gone, there was no reason for me to be listening to anything. A prospect was always on duty outside to give me a heads-up when the conman was coming and going.

However, I was curious...so I turned up the equipment I'd installed that covered the areas beyond Jeff's apartment.

A low, sultry voice floated into my ears, and to

my shock, my body stirred. I hadn't felt any interest in a woman in years, physically or otherwise. A relationship wasn't something I wanted, but I'd never been a hookup kind of guy. So the fact that I was responding to just a voice was bizarre.

My interest was piqued, so I turned up the volume dial and relaxed on the couch that I'd moved into the empty apartment so I would be comfortable during the hours of surveillance.

"Beau!" Violet cried out. *"Oh, oh! Oh, yes! Beau! Beau!"*

Bile rose in my throat, and a bitter taste saturated my mouth when I realized what I was hearing.

I was about to shut it off when her next words had me pausing.

Her voice shifted lower and took on a more masculine energy. *"'That's it, sweet girl,' I grunted. 'Fuck. I can't wait to feel this pussy wrapped around my cock. Oh, fuck, yeah. Fuck!'"*

What the hell?

"I curled my finger inside her and bit her clit, sending her into the stratosphere. Even though my orgasm had begun to ebb, hearing her set off another. This one was harder, and I had to shoot to my feet and lean over the desk so I wouldn't collapse on the floor.

My mouth found Isabella's, and she moaned

*when my tongue slid along hers and she tasted herself.
'See how amazing you taste?' I mumbled.*

I cupped her tits and used my thumbs to play with her nipples as I kissed down her neck. My cock hadn't gone very soft, and it was nearly fully hard again. As soon as she was ready, I was going to—"

My phone buzzing in my pocket jerked me out of the world Violet's voice had pulled me into.

I ripped off my headphones and yanked out my phone, stabbing the answer button before putting it to my ear. "Yeah?"

"Hey," greeted my club brother, Wizard. He was a tech genius and had earned his road name because he could make shit appear from thin air...which meant finding stuff no one else had been able to get their hands on, often by looking in places no one had ever thought to consider. "I've been tracking all of Jeff's accounts and was able to compile a list of former victims. Sending it to you in case he drops any info about them. Also, I'm still working on the accounts he transfers the money to. The account is constantly changing, and they're buried behind a fuck ton of aliases and shit. He's never given his cut from the same account either. Keep an ear out for anything he says about banking or former employers paying him, shit like that."

"Will do," I agreed.

We talked for another couple of minutes, analyzing some of the stuff Jeff had said over the past couple of days. Sometimes, things that sounded like useless bullshit were more helpful than others realized.

Violet was still on my mind during our conversation, and I hadn't come up with an explanation for what I'd heard. So before we hung up, I unexpectedly blurted out a request. "Need some information on his neighbor. Get a dossier together for me."

"Sure. You think she's involved?"

"No." I quickly tried to come up with an excuse that would make more sense than me being a stalker who was turned on by her voice but wouldn't implicate her in Jeff's activities. "She's got the best access to his place with the balconies next to each other and sharing a wall. If I can get on friendly terms with her, it would make getting the cameras in his place easier."

"Good idea. I'll send you some info today and get started on a deep dive. If she's got skeletons, you could use blackmail to get her cooperation."

The idea of doing something underhanded to get close to her didn't sit well with me...which was weird because it had never bothered me before. Not one of us would ever hurt someone innocent, especially a woman, but that hadn't stopped us from using subversive tactics to get what we needed.

"Just get me her information." I schooled my tone to make sure it was nonchalant when I added, "A picture would help."

"Yeah, then you'll recognize her if you see her outside the building first," he assumed.

"Right," I murmured, relieved that he'd come up with his own reason, rather than having to lie so he didn't know I simply wanted to see if Violet's looks matched her incredibly sexy voice.

We hung up, and I put on my headphones once again, listening to Violet speak and getting lost in her voice again.

"'For now, it's just you and me. Nobody and nothing else matters.'

'I like the sound of that,' I sighed, my cheeks heating.

'You're going to like the feel of it even more,' he promised, dropping our hands onto his lap and pressing my palm against his hard-on.

'Holy crap,' I whispered, wondering how he was ever going to possibly fit inside me.

As though he could read my mind, he chuckled. 'Don't worry, sweet girl. Just like I did when I had you spread out on my desk, I'm going to make tonight very, very good for you.'

Remembering the five mind-blowing orgasms he'd given me, my fingers flexed as my cheeks heated further. 'I'm sure you will.'"

Fucking hell. My body tingled from the overtly sexual tone in her words and voice.

A notification popped up on my computer screen, and I clicked open my email to see a message from Wizard.

I turned down the volume on my headset and opened the email, quickly downloading the attachment.

My intention was to look at her picture first, but for some reason, her occupation caught my attention.

Audiobook narrator.

Relief slithered through my body, and an amused smile curled my lips. I'd quickly realized I wasn't listening to Violet with another man, but it hadn't occurred to me that she was reading a book.

Considering how she'd pulled me in with her narration, she was obviously damn good at her job. However, it made me wonder if she would sound anything like her character when she was in the throes of real passion.

I skipped down the rest of the information and clicked on her picture, blowing it up on the screen.

Holy. Fucking. Shit.

The buzz of sexual chemistry I'd been feeling exploded into deep hunger, an almost overpowering desire to storm across the hall and fuck the unbelievably sexy woman from the photograph.

Violet stood next to a table where another woman sat, her head bent over a book as she signed it. There was a banner behind Violet with a book cover and "Narrator: Violet Kimball" printed just below the author's much larger name.

Violet's stunning eyes immediately caught my attention. I wondered if her parents had named her for their unique, deep purple color. Her long, dark brown hair floated around her, emphasizing her pale skin, making her eyes pop even more. Plush lips were spread out in a wide, beautiful smile, showing dimples digging into her plump cheeks.

I continued to study her photo, my eyes tracking down her body, and I licked my lips, my rock-hard cock twitching with excitement.

She was average height, no more than five foot four inches, but it was enough of a difference that I would tower over her at my six foot two inches.

I might have worried that my muscular frame

and tall stature would be too much for this dainty creature, but Violet had a full body with mouthwatering curves. Her big tits would spill out of my hands, and her wide hips would be perfect for holding while her thick thighs were wrapped around me. Although I couldn't see her ass in the picture, I had a feeling it was just as round and sexy as the rest of her.

Dragging my eyes away from her picture, I scanned the rest of the file and was not surprised to see Violet described as sweet, funny, and witty. There was just something about her that had told me she was the perfect fucking woman. And Jeff would never get near her again because she was mine.

2

VIOLET

Returning home after grocery shopping shouldn't be a big deal. But here I was, doing my best to walk down the hallway as quietly as possible. Unfortunately, I realized my efforts proved useless when my neighbor's door flung open when I was still a good fifty feet away from it.

I was too far away from the elevator to turn back but not close enough to my apartment to avoid talking to him. I barely held back an audible groan at seeing Jeff step out of his apartment.

He seemed to have an internal radar when it came to me. No matter how hard I tried to avoid him, he always seemed to be lurking anytime I left my apartment. Or returned.

If I didn't know better, I'd think he had a tracker of some kind on me.

"Hey, Jeff," I muttered, hefting one of the bags high enough to cover my chest so he couldn't leer at my boobs.

"Hi, Violet. Do you need some help carrying that stuff?" he offered, his gaze raking down my body, sending a cold shiver along my spine.

I shook my head and grimaced. "No thanks, I have it."

If he had been any of my other neighbors, I would have taken him up on the offer, but I learned quickly that Jeff was the kind of guy who took a mile if you gave him an inch. Which was probably why he was single even though he was handsome enough to attract plenty of feminine attention with his blond hair, blue eyes, and runner's physique.

I didn't understand why he was so fixated on me unless it was because his good looks had never pulled me in. Maybe he was one of those guys who liked the challenge. Whatever the reason, I'd give just about anything for him to forget I existed.

"Oh, okay." His shoulders slumped. "Let me know if you ever need anything. I'm right next door, only a wall away."

"Yep, I know."

His proximity was the only reason I was considering not renewing my lease for another year. My apartment was perfect for me in every way but one—Jeff.

I loved the balcony looking over the woods that lined the back of the complex. And the walk-in closet in my second bedroom had been easy to convert into the vocal booth where I did my voiceover work, mostly recording audiobooks. The kitchen was also great, with granite countertops and more cabinet space than I knew what to do with.

Finding another place with the same amenities without a huge hike in rent would be tough, but I wasn't sure I wanted to spend another year afraid to leave my apartment. Working from home meant that I didn't get a lot of interaction with people during the day, so it would've been nice to be able to get out more often without having to worry about running into Jeff. Having him as a neighbor had turned me into a hermit instead of just an introvert.

He stepped closer as I struggled with sticking my key into the lock while holding two overly full bags. "Are you sure you don't need help?"

"Whatever Violet needs, I have it covered."

My head swung up at the deep voice, and I was stunned by who I found walking toward us. If I had asked my favorite client to write the description of my fantasy guy, she couldn't have done any better than the man standing in front of me. He looked as though he had come to life from the pages of a motorcycle club romance book.

Except for the fact that he was a ginger because I didn't often run into book boyfriends with red hair. I would definitely need to search them out from now on, though, because he was sexier than any man had the right to be.

He was tall and muscular in a way that made me think he earned his build outside of the gym. His hair was a deep red, and his close-cropped beard was the same color. His blue eyes reminded me of the ocean when I took a snorkeling trip in the Bahamas. With his short sleeve shirt under his Hounds of Hellfire cut, I could see most of the full sleeve of black ink on his left arm.

I'd never seen him in the building before...and he was definitely someone I'd remember. That was probably because I hadn't done a great job of getting to know my neighbors since I tended to rush through the lobby in my attempts to avoid Jeff.

But that didn't stop me from going along with him when he tugged both bags out of my arms and flashed me a sexy smile. "Sorry it took me so long to park the car, baby."

"Who the hell are you?" Jeff demanded, glaring at the guy.

He turned to my neighbor, juggling the bags so he was holding them in one arm while he slid the other behind my back to pull me against his side. "I'm her boyfriend, Echo."

"Violet doesn't have a boyfriend," Jeff argued, his eyes going wide.

Echo quirked a brow. "Not sure why you think you're close enough to my girl to be in the loop on what's going on in her life."

"I keep an eye out for her. Make sure she's safe." Jeff puffed out his chest. "And I've never seen you around here before."

"Unless you're watching her twenty-four seven, then you're bound to miss shit. Like me being in her life." Echo shrugged. "Appreciate you looking out for my girl, but I have her covered from here. You can consider yourself relieved of duty."

I shoved the key in the lock and yanked open the door before Jeff had the chance to reply. Then I tugged Echo into my apartment and slammed the door shut behind us. Turning to the sexy biker, I pressed a trembling hand against my chest. "Thank you so much for stepping in like that. Jeff was being even pushier than usual. I'm not sure how I would've convinced him that I didn't need help getting my door unlocked while trying to juggle my groceries. And the last thing I want is him inside my apartment."

"Happy to help." His lips curved into a grin as he shifted one of the bags to his free arm. "Where do you want 'em?"

"Oh, um...just in the kitchen." I was about to offer to take them from Echo when I glanced at the door and realized that if I rushed him out of my apartment, Jeff would get suspicious about him being my boyfriend. "Thanks."

I followed him through the living room, relieved I'd cleaned this morning before heading out to run errands. Since I spent most of my time at home, the place usually looked very well lived in, but I had put most of the clutter away.

Echo's biceps flexed as he placed the bags on the island and started to pull out the items I'd purchased. "You don't need to do that. I have it."

He stepped to the side, making room for me in the narrow space between the island and the stove and fridge. His focus remained on me while I emptied the bags and put everything away. "You a good baker?"

"I like to think so."

My cheeks heated at the timing of him being in my apartment. Of course it had to happen when I did my quarterly restock of my baking supplies. A lot of people would've said something snide about how I didn't need to eat stuff with the sugar, chocolate chips, and butter I'd bought. But Echo's blue eyes heated as his gaze traveled down my curves.

"You know how to make brownies?" he asked.

I nodded. "Yup, but I'm a purist when it comes to them. They have to be fudgy, without anything extra like nuts, chocolate chips, or frosting."

He chuckled, the deep sound sending a shiver of awareness down my spine. "I like 'em however the chef wants to make them."

"I should bake you a batch as a thank you for rescuing me, Echo."

"I wouldn't turn them down," he assured me. "But call me Brodie. Echo's my road name."

"Then I guess I know what I'll be doing this afternoon, Brodie." I padded over to the door and peered through the peephole. "The coast is clear. You should be good to head back to your apartment without Jeff seeing you. Just let me know which number you are so I can bring you those brownies later."

"Appreciate you looking out for me." His lips curved into a grin as he shrugged. "But I don't live here."

"You don't?" I asked, my brows drawing together.

"Nope," he confirmed with a shake of his head. "I was just in the right place at the right time to swoop in and rescue you."

"Lucky me." I probably should've felt at risk having a strange man in my apartment, but something about his presence was comforting.

"Glad you think so since I'm in this for the long haul. I hope you're ready for our relationship to move to the next level because I'm moving in."

3

ECHO

"Moving in?" Violet squeaked, her hands fluttering at her sides.

Satisfaction swept through me when I didn't see a speck of fear in her gaze. There was apprehension but also a spark of excitement. I was confident that she felt the same chemistry as I did when I touched her.

I nodded as I took a step closer to her. "I need you."

Violet's breathing kicked up, and I held back a wicked smile. "Need me?"

I didn't want to scare her away by going too fast, so I backed off even though it was the opposite of what I wanted to do. "I need your help to take down that asshole."

Violet's brow furrowed, and she cocked her head to the side. "Pardon? Take down Jeff?"

"Yeah. He's dangerous, and he's fucked over the wrong people. We're gonna nail his ass to the wall, and it will go a fuck of a lot faster if I'm as close to him as possible."

She raised her eyebrows and pointed at the floor. "Here?"

Grinning, I took a step closer, forcing her back against the counter, then caged her in by resting a hand on both sides. "Can't get any closer than next door, and you've given me the perfect opportunity. I'm thinking it's a fair trade," I said with a wink.

"A trade for what?"

"I get to use your proximity to your neighbor, and you get him to stay away from you by thinking you have a live-in boyfriend."

"I see your point," she conceded.

My smile faded, replaced by a frown as I explained the situation. "Jeff is a conman. He's been preying on women with money, getting close and then stealing everything they've got."

Violet rubbed her lips together as she digested what I'd told her. "No wonder I always got such a creepy vibe from him when he hit on me," she murmured.

My hands clenched into fists at her comment. It wasn't like I hadn't known he was pursuing her, but it still made me furious to hear it out loud.

Her expression turned puzzled, and she asked, "But why is he bothering with me? I'm not rich."

I hesitated to tell her my conclusion, knowing it would probably freak her out. Still, it honestly seemed the best route, especially if it kept her guard up around Jeff.

"I don't think it's about money, baby," I told her softly.

"What else could it be?" Her genuine confusion made me frown. Didn't she know how gorgeous she was?

I gestured up and down her body. "Your sexy-as-fuck body, for starters."

Violet's cheeks turned adorably red as she dropped her eyes to my chest. "It's not that I'm unhappy with how I look. But I don't think guys..."

She trailed off when I put a finger beneath her chin and raised her head so she was staring at my face. "*Trust me*, Violet."

Her blush deepened, and her dimples appeared, her eyes sparkling with pleasure when she nodded. "Okay." After a few seconds, her nose wrinkled as her expression soured. "You think he wants to date me? Ew."

I chuckled and barely resisted the urge to brush a kiss across her plump lips. "Don't worry. I won't let him get near you."

Violet's eyes swept down my body before meeting mine again, and she snickered, her smile making her sexy dimples deepen. "I doubt he'll try anything if he thinks you're my man." Damn, I loved the sound of that. "I mean...a huge, badass, sexy biker guy seems like the sort he would run away from."

"You think I'm sexy?" I asked with a smirk.

She scoffed, "Like you don't know that. I'm sure you have women falling all over themselves to be with you."

"Only interested in what you think, baby. Don't give a fuck about anyone else." I grinned when she blushed again and teased, "I'll trust you not to try to take advantage of me while I'm crashing here."

"So you can get evidence to get Jeff arrested?"

"Actually, we've already got enough on him to put him in jail, but we recently realized he's not the one calling the shots. We set up surveillance so we can get access to the big fish."

Violet nodded. "That makes sense. Sort of."

"Sort of?"

"Needing my apartment to get close to Jeff...that makes sense." She looked bewildered when she continued, "It doesn't make sense that I'm actually going to let a stranger move into my apartment." Her shoulders bounced in a shrug. "Or why I feel so safe with you after meeting you less than ten minutes ago."

I wanted to tell her it was because she was mine, but I'd wait until I'd moved my shit in so it would be harder for her to run from me.

"Good instincts."

Violet smiled. "I hope so."

Reluctantly, I shoved away from the counter and took a few steps back. "I need to go get my shit. If Jeff comes over after I leave, don't open the door. I'll deal with him when I get back."

She nodded, and I pressed my lips together, telling myself it was too soon to kiss her and spun around. "Lock up behind me," I called over my shoulder as I marched out of the kitchen and over to the front door.

When I was in the hallway, I waited to hear the click of her deadbolt sliding into place and shot a threatening glance at Jeff's door in case he was looking through his peephole.

I'd parked my bike in the lot next door, so once I

walked outside, I made a beeline for my ride. It only took ten minutes to reach the compound, and I put my motorcycle in the garage since I intended to take my Jeep back to Violet's place.

When I strolled into the clubhouse, my vice president, Blaze, was in the lounge with his old lady, Courtney.

"Didn't expect to see you around today," Blaze said with a raised eyebrow. "Thought you were gonna be busy with that"—he shot a look at Courtney and chose his words carefully since my activities were club business—"situation you were handling."

"Had to come in and grab some shit because I'm moving in with my woman today," I explained as I continued stalking across the room.

"Your woman?" Blaze echoed.

"Long story, man." I slapped him on the back as I passed by. "But don't worry, she's not gonna interfere with what I have to get done. In fact, it's the opposite."

Before he could inquire further, I disappeared down a hallway leading to a section of the first floor with rooms for club brothers to stay or live in. They were reminiscent of a dorm with a bed and sitting area, but the ones intended for permanent living space also had private bathrooms.

Since I was single and the club's road captain, it hadn't made sense for me to live in my own place. That was gonna change now that I'd met Violet, but I'd deal with it after we caught the head of the con ring.

When I reached my room, I unlocked it and opened the door, flicking the switch on the wall to turn on the lights. I had a black duffel bag stowed in my closet, so I grabbed it and shoved clothes and underwear inside before adding my toiletries.

I was already wearing my gun, but I had a backup piece in a safe on the top shelf of the closet. It was disassembled and in a case, so I entered the combination and took it out, adding the weapon to the duffel. I wanted Violet to have a gun in her apartment for when I was gone. If she didn't have a safe, I'd order one so I could keep it assembled. I had a feeling she didn't know how to shoot one, but in an emergency, all she had to know was point and click.

After everything was packed, I zipped up the bag and slung it over my shoulder, then stepped into the hall and locked my door. Hurrying down the hall, I heard more voices in the lounge. King stood just inside the front entrance with his woman, Stella. He held an infant carrier, and several people gathered around oohing and aahing over their newborn baby boy.

"Congrats, Prez," I murmured as I approached them.

"Thanks," he replied with a giant grin.

"Need to give you an update," I said in a low tone.

He nodded and bent to give his old lady a kiss before setting the baby on the nearest couch. "You good for a few minutes?" he asked her.

She glanced at me, then back at him and nodded. "Of course."

King and Blaze had both won the jackpot with their women. They were strong and independent but understood club life and their place in it. There would always be things they wouldn't know about, and in front of most other clubs, they played the submissive, obedient role. Otherwise, they were spitfires who gave as good as they got. My instincts told me that Violet would fit right in with them.

I followed King to his office and wasn't surprised to find Blaze right behind us. The prez leaned back against the front of his desk and crossed his arms over his chest. "Where are we at?"

Quickly, I filled them in on the developments,

and when I was done, King was smirking at me—somehow visible through his perpetual scowl. "You needed to be closer to Jeff?"

I shrugged as I confessed, "Not gonna pretend there wasn't another ulterior motive."

"Figured," Blaze said with a chuckle.

Glancing at him, I tilted my head and asked, "Think you could add a vest to your order for Courtney?"

King grunted, his expression somewhat amused. "I'm thinking we should start doing what some of our allies have done and just order a stash to have at the clubhouse."

Blaze grinned. "Probably a good idea. Need to find a local place to do the patches and embroidery, though. I..."

I stopped listening and gave them a wave—which was returned by a lift of their chins—and headed back to my woman.

4

VIOLET

Ten minutes after Brodie left, my head was still spinning. I wasn't surprised that Jeff was the kind of guy who took advantage of women, but I was stunned that his crimes had brought a sexy biker to my doorstep.

I wasn't angry about that part, though.

It was hard to imagine different circumstances that would have resulted in us meeting. I was a book-loving introvert who mostly stayed home—and not just because of my creepy neighbor. Brodie struck me as the kind of guy with a more active lifestyle than me. One that probably involved stuff like going to bars, which I couldn't even do if I wanted to since I was only twenty.

Or maybe I was making incorrect assumptions

about Brodie because he was in a motorcycle club. For all I knew, he liked to stay in and read as much as I did.

My eyes widened as my gaze darted toward the bookshelf in my living room. It was full of spicy romance novels, something we probably didn't have in common since I couldn't picture a guy like him reading about heroines who don't need to choose between three or four guys who all want to worship her. Or fictional motorcycle clubs that he'd probably cringe over because he belonged to a real one.

I couldn't do much about the rows of paperbacks on my shelves before he came back. I didn't have anywhere else to put them all, and the bookcase would look odd if it was empty. Which would only draw more attention to my reading preferences.

Instead, I decided to use my time wisely and focus on cleaning the spaces he hadn't seen yet. Rushing into my bedroom, I grabbed the randomly strewn clothes from the floor and tossed them into the laundry basket in my closet. Then I stripped the bed before grabbing the spare set of sheets from the linen closet.

There wasn't a bed in the other room, so Brodie would need to use my bed, and fresh sheets were a must since it'd been ten days since I'd changed them.

Normally, I did them every week, but I'd skipped my most recent laundry day while racing toward a deadline for the book I finished this morning.

Thank goodness that was done...I couldn't imagine recording sexy scenes like the ones my best client wrote while Brodie was in the apartment. Even with the soundproofing in my recording booth, I'd be way too aware of his presence not to stumble over my words.

Time literally was money for me. I had a long list of pending projects, so the faster I could record a book, the more I could take on. Luckily, the manuscript I was supposed to work on next was a slow burn, so I didn't need to worry about recording a sex scene while he was in the next room.

I had managed to clean the bathroom, empty a dresser drawer, and make some space in my closet when I heard Brodie's knock. Running my fingers through my hair, I took a deep breath before pulling open the door with a smile. "Hey." I glanced down at the single bag clutched in his fist. "You packed fast and light."

"Don't need much personal stuff." He waited until he was inside the apartment with the door shut behind him to add, "But I have some surveillance equipment I'll need to set up."

"Hmm." I pressed my lips together as I considered the best spot for him to put that kind of stuff. "Do you need to use the shared wall between our apartments?"

He shook his head. "Nah, you can put me wherever you want. My shit won't take up a lot of space."

I pointed toward the oversized chair in the corner of the room. "You can scoot that over by the couch if you want."

He glanced over there, his lips curving into a grin. "I think my stuff will fit on that circular table next to it, and I can use the chair while I'm listening to what Jeff has going on while he's home. With me in that corner, you'll barely know I'm here."

Shaking my head, I giggled. "I doubt that would ever be possible."

His eyes held a glimmer of masculine satisfaction as he asked, "Should I take that as a compliment?"

"Definitely," I whispered, fiddling with the hem of my shirt as I gestured toward the hallway that led to the bedrooms, hoping to direct his attention away from my heated cheeks. "Want a quick tour of the place before you grab that equipment? Just in case there's somewhere that will work better."

"Sure, baby. Whatever you want to do."

Since climbing his body like a tree wasn't possible, I led him around my apartment instead. "You've already seen the living room and kitchen. The groceries I bought today should last us a little while since I was planning to make an extra lasagna for the freezer. Unless there's anything special you need?"

"I'm not picky," he assured me, patting his flat stomach with his free hand. "Anything you want to feed me, I'll eat."

My cheeks grew even hotter as an image of me feeding him my rounded tit popped in my head. "Ahh, good to know."

At his deep chuckle, I ducked my head and padded toward the hallway, pointing across the living room along the way. "The sliding glass door leads to the balcony. I have a couple of chairs and a small table out there, but I rarely use them since nothing is blocking Jeff's view out there."

"Won't have to worry about him for much longer," he growled, following me close.

I pointed out the guest bathroom before pulling the soundproofing blanket hiding the second bedroom door to the side. "Unfortunately, I don't have a bed in here for you to use. I'm an audiobook narrator, and I set this room up as my recording booth. I had to limit the furniture because of how sound echoes off hard surfaces."

Brodie moved the blanket on the other side of the door to look inside. "This is cool as fuck."

"Really?" I beamed a smile at him as he turned toward me. "It isn't super fancy because I did it all myself."

"I know more than a fair bit about audio equipment, and from what I can see, you did a kick-ass job."

Brodie was the first person who'd seen the booth I had created, and his compliment meant a lot to me. "Thanks."

"Just called it like I saw it."

He was careful with the blankets as he put them back into position, then we walked through the door at the end of the hallway. "Since you're so much bigger than me, you should take the bed. It's only a queen, but it's got to be more than twice the size of my couch. So I'll take that."

"Not gonna happen, baby." He dropped his black duffel near the closet door and turned toward me, crossing his arms over his broad chest. "No way in hell am I gonna kick you out of your bed."

My nose scrunched. "You won't get much sleep on my couch, though."

He looked at my bed. "With how tiny you are, a

queen-sized mattress is plenty of space for both of us."

Rolling my eyes, I shook my head. "I'm the furthest thing from tiny."

"Only in the places where a man wants his woman to have curves." His eyes heated as his gaze raked down my body. "It'll be hell keeping my hands off you, but I swear you have nothing to fear from me. I'd never touch you unless I knew damn well that you wanted it. But if you're not comfortable sharing a bed with me, I'll be fine in the living room. I slept in lots of worse places during my time in the Marines."

There was no doubting the sincerity shining from his eyes. My gut told me that I could trust Brodie...it was my own self-control that I was worried about. "We can share."

"Good." He gestured toward his bag. "I'll take care of that after I bring in my equipment. Gotta get that done while Jeff is out so he doesn't know I'm listening in."

"Sounds like we have a plan." I followed him down the hall, detouring to the kitchen when he headed for the door. "While you're taking care of all that, I'll get to work on that lasagna. And those brownies I owe you."

Pausing with his hand on the knob, he looked at me over his shoulder. "I'm not gonna turn down anything you want to bake, but you've more than paid me back for steppin' in with Jeff by letting me stay with you."

"Then maybe I'll make them just because."

"Works for me," he grunted.

I fanned myself with my hand after he walked out, whispering, "Holy heck, that man is too hot for my own good."

By the time he was settled into my place with his equipment set up, the lasagnas were in the oven, and a pan of brownies was ready to pop in once dinner was done.

"Do you mind if we eat at the island?" I pointed at the small, rectangular table that was pushed against the wall, with two chairs tucked underneath. "I hardly ever use that."

"You'll never get a complaint from me when you're serving a home-cooked meal." He stalked over to the sink and gently nudged me out of the way. "Except for when it comes to cleaning up. You cooked, so I'll take care of this."

I lifted my hands in a gesture of surrender. "You won't get any arguments from me. I hate doing dishes."

"Good thing you don't need to worry about them from now on, then."

It was going to be rough to go back to doing them myself when he was gone, but I had a feeling that wasn't the only thing I would miss about him. Including having someone to share meals with.

I enjoyed watching him devour the plate of lasagna and bowl of salad that I served him less than an hour later. And the second helping.

When we were done, I put away the leftovers while he cleaned our dishes. Then we moved to the living room to eat our dessert and get to know each other a little better.

I was blown away when he said, "Gotta admit, I already knew you were an audiobook narrator."

"You did?" I tilted my head to the side and asked, "How?"

He jerked his chin toward the equipment he'd stacked near my oversized chair. "Picked up audio of you recording a scene. Confused the fuck outta me at first. I thought you were in here with someone until you did the guy's lines."

"Oh my gosh," I whispered when I realized what he might've heard,

"Never read a romance book before, but I can see how you can afford this place. It was hot as fuck."

"And on that note, I should probably get ready for bed." I stood and gave an exaggerated yawn. "It's been quite the day."

"Go ahead, baby. I'll wait until you're done."

Going to sleep with Brodie only inches away from me ended up being easier than I expected. For the first time since Jeff's interest in me became obvious, I felt safe in my own home. And that allowed me to drift off to sleep within minutes…where I dreamed about the man who'd somehow already made a place for himself in my life.

5

ECHO

Violet had shelves and shelves of romance novels, but I seriously doubted that any one of those authors could truly capture the perfection of waking up with Violet in my arms.

A few minutes after she'd drifted off last night, she'd rolled over and snuggled her sexy body up against mine. I'd already been stiff with desire, but when I turned onto my side so her back was to my front, her big, round ass cradled my cock, and I went rock fucking hard. I put one arm under her head and curled the other around her waist, resting my palm on her soft belly. It had been the best night's sleep I'd ever had—even with the dirty dreams that had me waking up with an aching shaft several times throughout the night.

When I woke up, I was instantly in heaven and hell.

Violet was plastered against my body, leaving no space between us. The arm I'd had under her head was crooked over her shoulder and into the wide neck of her T-shirt, my hand filled with her bare tit.

My knee was bent between her thighs, and her top leg was flung back over mine. The position opened her up so that my other hand was cupping her pussy over her sleep shorts.

The thin cotton was soaked, and the heat of her center was practically scorching. My fingers flexed involuntarily, and I froze when a soft moan fell from her lips.

Son of a bitch. If I didn't let her go right now, I was gonna lose my shit and fuck Violet less than a day after meeting her. I might have gained a good portion of her trust, but I didn't think shoving my dick inside her so soon would build up more.

"Brodie," she sighed, wiggling her ass back against the long, thick rod digging into her back.

"Shit, shit, shit," I muttered, silently yelling at myself to roll away.

Then her pelvis bucked and her back arched, pressing her into my hands as another moan fell from her lips.

"Violet," I gritted in her ear. "You need to stop, baby."

"No," she whined.

I squeezed my eyes shut and breathed deeply, but it only filled my lungs with her delicious scent. The sweet, sugary smell was now permeated with the musky tang of her arousal.

"Baby," I growled. I wasn't sure if she was awake, so I spoke with a little more force this time. "You gotta move away from me before I lose control. I'm barely hanging on by a thread, and if you don't stop me, I'm gonna fuck you."

Violet's leg shifted higher up my leg, giving me even more access to her pussy, while she lifted a hand to my neck and gently scored her nails down the skin. "What if that's what I want?"

Her voice was breathy, and my hands flexed again. This time, my middle finger pushed against the fabric of her shorts, nestling between the lips of her pussy and rubbing the cloth over her clit.

She cried out, and her nipples became diamond-hard tips, one scraping my palm as she pushed it deeper into my hand.

"Fuck," I grunted. After giving the globe a strong squeeze, I pinched and plucked the stiff peak while I shoved my other hand into her shorts so I could play with her naked center. "Fucking drenched," I groaned. "Were you dreaming about this, baby?"

"Yes," she whispered.

"Did you imagine me inside you?" I asked as I slowly penetrated her with one finger.

"Yes!" she hissed, bringing her leg down so my hand was trapped between her thighs.

"No," I growled, shoving her leg back up. "You stay where I tell you, or I stop. Is that clear?"

She turned her head and stared up at me with lust-glazed eyes and bit her lip as she nodded.

"Good girl. Now keep them open, I want to play with this wet pussy." I bent my head and took her lips in a deep kiss while I swirled my fingers around her clit and dipped them into her channel.

She was tight as hell, and I wondered, "Violet? Baby, are you a virgin?"

Violet froze, and her purple orbs filled with worry as she met my gaze. "Yes," she murmured.

"Fucking hell," I grunted as I dropped my head so our foreheads were touching.

"Please don't stop."

Her plea had me flipping her onto her back so I hovered over her, our gazes locked. "Couldn't even if

I wanted to. I'm already addicted, but knowing you're untouched? That I'm the only man who will ever be inside you...fuck, baby. You've sealed your fate, Violet. You're mine."

I didn't wait for a response before claiming her mouth. A groan rumbled in my chest when her lips parted, and my tongue plunged inside. She tasted as sweet as she smelled, with a flavor that was all her own.

She threw herself into the kiss, and her enthusiastic response rapidly disintegrated my control.

Now that I knew how inexperienced she was, I would have to slow down and be more careful with her.

Shifting to my knees, I inhaled and exhaled slowly, peeling her shirt up and forcing her to raise her arms so I could take it off.

When her arms dropped to the bed, my breath got caught in my throat as I watched her generous tits bounce. My mouth watered, but I was distracted when she ran the fingertips of one hand up my torso before touching the small silver hoop in my right nipple.

"I've read about piercings in my books, but I never realized just how sexy they were," she confessed breathlessly.

"You can't say shit like that to me right now," I grunted.

Mentioning her books made me curious, though. I wondered if she'd read about things she would want to experience. It could be a whole lotta fun finding new, interesting ways to bring each other pleasure. "What else have you read about?"

Before she could answer, I shook my head. "Don't answer that. I don't think I can handle it right now."

Violet giggled. "I'll make you a list later."

"Perfect," I told her with a smirk. "We'll call it...research."

"Okay." Her voice was breathy, and my cock throbbed as I glided my hands down her torso, over her soft belly, and crooked my fingers into the waistband of her shorts. Slowly, I dragged them south, and when I revealed her center, my breath caught in my lungs. My world halted as I took in the beauty of my girl's sweet, bare, virgin pussy.

I licked my lips, already salivating at the idea of tasting her there.

Quickly, I stood next to the bed and yanked her shorts all the way off. Then I pulled off my boxers and climbed back onto the mattress, settling on my stomach between her legs. I pushed them as wide as they would go, then used my thumbs to part her dewy lips and stared at her swollen pink perfection.

"Gorgeous," I murmured before dropping my head so my face was buried in her center as I inhaled deeply. "You smell so fucking good."

My tongue slid over her clit, and I used the weight of my arms on her legs to keep her pelvis from rocking up. "I'm in charge, baby," I warned her again. Then I dragged my tongue from the tip of her pussy to her bottom and back up. I lapped at her sensitive flesh until she was crying out my name and writhing in passion.

It only took me a minute to have her hands grasping my hair while she begged me to give her release. I pushed her over the edge, but I kept devouring her like a starving man, giving her two more orgasms before I let her have a respite.

"That was..." she sighed, her hands plunging into her own hair and yanking on the strands as her body vibrated with aftershocks. "I'm..."

"Need you to be ready for me, baby," I rasped as I crawled up her body. "Hate to hurt you, but I can't stop it when I'm popping your cherry. The more relaxed you are, the easier it will be."

"I don't think I can take any more," she whined softly.

I grinned and kissed the tip of her nose. "Trust me, baby. You can take all of me."

Violet snickered. "That's not what I meant."

"Give me your mouth, Violet," I demanded, my tone firm but gentle.

She raised her head, and I slammed my lips down onto hers. The fingers of one hand wrapped around her hip while the other went into her silky brown tresses. I pulled hard enough to draw her head back, opening her mouth so I could sweep my tongue inside, letting her taste her own sweetness.

"Fuck, I need to be inside you," I groaned.

"Yesss," she hissed, her legs coming up to wrap around my hips.

I positioned my tip at her entrance and paused, resting my forehead on hers for a moment. It took a second for my heart to stop pounding so hard. I was afraid it would burst through my chest. When it did, I captured Violet's mouth once more, waiting for her to throw herself into the kiss before I thrust fast and deep until I was sheathed in her tight channel.

"Fuck!" I shouted, throwing my head back in ecstasy when her walls clenched around me.

I froze when I heard a little sniff, and my head snapped up, my eyes flying open. "Shit. Are you okay, baby?" I asked, terrified that I'd torn her open or something. She was tiny compared to me, especially in *that* department.

"I'm...I'm okay," she whispered. Her purple eyes glistened with tears, but the pain in their depths was slowly dissipating. "I just needed to...um...stretch. You're really big, you know."

Chuckling, I rub my nose over hers. "Told you, baby. Can't say shit like that to me unless you want me to fuck your brains out."

"Probably not a good idea this time, but can I get a rain check?"

I burst into laughter this time, and if it hadn't caused me to slide in a little deeper, I might have taken a second to appreciate that this perfect woman could make me hot as hell and happy enough to laugh heartily, all at the same time.

But rational thought shot out of my brain, and I moaned as I glided backward before sliding back in. "Oh fuck," I muttered. Sparks of pleasure exploded from my nerve endings, and my cock throbbed with need.

"You gotta come, baby," I said through clenched teeth. "I can't hold back much longer."

"Don't," she whispered. "Don't hold back with me."

Something inside me broke free and took over. Nothing was left but the mating instinct, the urgent need to fill my woman with my come, to make her scream my name, to take her to the breaking point of pleasure and spiral down together.

"Brodie," she moaned. "Yes. Oh yes!"

A sound outside the window sent a sliver of reality racing into my brain. I didn't want anyone hearing my woman find her pleasure. "You gotta keep quiet, baby," I muttered. "Just the thought of another man hearing you come makes me fucking homicidal."

Violet's pussy clenched, and I grunted, "That make you hot, Violet? Knowing I'd kill for you?"

"It probably shouldn't," she admitted with a gasp as I slammed in deep enough to bump her cervix.

"Nothing is wrong when it's between you and me, baby."

"I need you, Brodie," she moaned. "Yes! Yes! Brodie!"

"Quiet," I grunted. "I love hearing how I make you feel, baby. I don't want to stop, but you gotta keep it down, or I will."

Violet pressed her lips together and nodded. When I rammed into her twice more and she didn't make a sound, I kissed her and mumbled, "Good girl," against her mouth.

"Fuck, baby. Take all that cock. Oh, fuck."

Grabbing her big, sexy ass, I yanked her hips up as I got to my knees and stared down in rapture as I watched my shaft disappear inside her over and over.

"I'm gonna come," she choked out, and I petted her pussy softly.

"Such a good girl," I praised because she'd kept her voice restrained. With just the tip of a finger, I circled her clit while I continued to pound inside her. Then I slid my finger over the bundle of nerves before rubbing it intensely.

Her legs began to shake as her climax clawed to the surface. When I saw she was about to let go, I slapped my hand over her mouth, then I tossed my head back in a silent roar as we came together.

White light flashed before my eyes, and hot streaks of pleasure sliced through my body as I filled her with my seed.

When my breathing began to slow, I collapsed on top of her and grunted, "Fuck, that was amazing."

Violet nodded, her purple orbs staring at the ceiling, still hazy from her passionate orgasm.

"Ever read about a virgin getting her cherry popped?" I teased.

"I can't imagine a hero in a book ever making me feel the way you do, Brodie," she sighed.

My heart squeezed, and I swallowed hard, overwhelmed with emotion. Finally, I kissed her softly and whispered, "No fantasy could ever live up to you, baby."

6

VIOLET

I was usually more of a night person, but starting my morning by giving Brodie my virginity had given me so much energy that I felt as though I could tackle my entire month's to-do list all in one day. Toying with the small hoop ring through his right nipple, I tilted my head back to smile at him.

"I had no idea that orgasms are better than coffee."

He stroked his palm down my spine to cup my butt cheek. "Anytime you want one instead of caffeine to give you a boost, let me know. I'll provide you with as many orgasms as you need, whenever you want 'em."

"I will definitely keep that offer in mind." I

squeezed my thighs together, feeling a slight ache where he'd just been with a slight wince.

"After you recover." He brushed his lips against my temple. "Hurting you when I popped your cherry couldn't be avoided, but I'm not gonna do that again by taking you too soon."

I appreciated how in tune he seemed to be with what I thought and felt, putting his observation skills to use for my benefit. "Nothing a nice hot bath won't cure."

"I'll run one for you." He dropped a quick kiss on my mouth before sliding out of bed. Smiling down at me, he asked, "Do you have any girly shit you want me to put in the water?"

I nodded, laughing softly. "Yeah, I have a bunch of stuff in the cabinet under the sink. Pick whatever you want to dump in there. And I like my baths extra hot."

"Will do, baby."

I cuddled against the pillow he used last night, pressing my nose into the cover and dragging his woodsy scent deep into my lungs. It was too bad that all of my toiletries smelled like flowers or fruit because I would've happily walked around surrounded by Brodie's scent all day.

When I heard the shower turn on, I made a

mental note to check in there to see if he brought his own body wash. If so, I was going to borrow it at some point. And maybe buy a bottle for myself... or a dozen since I was already addicted to his smell.

I must've drifted off again because the next thing I knew, Brodie lifted me off the mattress to carry me into the bathroom. The tub was already full, and he dipped one of my toes into the water before asking, "Temp okay?"

"It's perfect," I murmured, rubbing my cheek against his bare chest.

"Careful, baby." He set me in the tub, and I rested my head against the rolled-up towel he'd put on one end.

The citrus scent of my favorite bath salts hit my nose. "Mmm, exactly what I needed."

"I'll check on you in a little bit; make sure you don't fall asleep."

"Good idea." I smiled up at him. "Too bad you're so big, or else I'd suggest you join me in here."

"That'd defeat the purpose of the bath, baby." He crouched down and tugged on a lock of my hair. "You and me, naked in a tub together, would end up with lots of orgasms your tight pussy isn't ready for yet."

"Stupid virginity," I muttered with a pout. "If I'd gotten rid of it before—"

"Don't," he growled before capturing my lips in a punishing kiss that left me breathless. "That cherry was mine, just like every other part of you."

I gently pushed against his shoulders. "You better stop with that caveman talk unless you want me to pull you in here with me."

"You have no idea how much I want that," he groaned, standing again. "But unfortunately, I gotta do what's best for you. Stop tempting me and take your bath."

"Yes, sir." I winked at him and giggled, making him shake his head with a sigh.

"Fucking hell," he muttered as he strode out of the bathroom.

Finally realizing that the only thing he had on was the towel wrapped around his waist, I gasped. "Stupid sleepy brain. I didn't even really get to enjoy the view."

I must've been louder than I thought—or he just had great hearing—because he called, "Don't worry, baby. You'll have plenty of other chances to look as much as you want."

"I better," I muttered to myself as I slid deeper into the hot water, determined to let the salts work their magic on my muscles so I could do something about how sexy he was when I next had the chance.

Thirty minutes later when I climbed out of the tub—after he had checked on me twice—I had to admit Brodie had been right. I really had needed to give my body the chance to recover from losing my virginity to him. I felt so much better, without any twinges as I got dressed.

Brodie was fiddling with his surveillance equipment when I walked into the living room. "Hungry?"

"Famished."

His rakish smile made me think he wasn't just talking about food, but the rumble of my stomach made me focus on breakfast before I tried to talk him into testing out how much the bath helped my sore pussy.

"Any special requests?" I asked.

"After what you fed me yesterday, I'm going with chef's choice."

I rubbed my palms together with a smile. "Excellent."

I dug through the fridge and pantry to pull out the ingredients I needed for one of my favorite breakfast dishes, quiche. I rarely bothered to make one since it was a lot of effort for just one person. But

Brodie had a hearty appetite—in and out of bed—and I wanted to impress him.

Luckily, I had a homemade butter crust in the freezer from the last time I baked a pie since it was easier to make a big batch and save the extra crusts for later. All I had to do was pop it in the oven for ten minutes while I prepared the quiche base. Since I was feeding Brodie, I went heavy on the meat, adding about double the amount of chopped ham than I would normally use, along with a lot of freshly grated cheddar cheese.

While it was in the oven, I made a pot of coffee and chopped some fresh fruit. Brodie joined me in the kitchen when the timer went off, and I pulled out the pie pan.

"Lasagna and brownies last night and quiche for breakfast?" He wrapped his arms around my waist, pressing his chest against my back as he peered over my shoulder. "You're gonna spoil me, baby."

I twisted my neck to grin up at him. "Considering all of the orgasms you gave me, I think the same could be said for you."

After brushing his lips against my neck, he stepped back and patted his six-pack abs. "If you keep feeding me like this, I'm gonna have to work out more."

Turning around, I wagged my brows. "I can think of a fun way to burn off calories."

"Are we exchanging food for orgasms?" he asked with a laugh.

I shrugged. "Hey, a girl's gotta do what a girl's gotta do."

Cupping my chin, he swiped his thumb across my cheek. "Meant it when I said I'd give you as many orgasms as you want, baby. No paybacks necessary."

"I mean…I can also think of fun ways to pay you back. Like making you come, too."

He tugged me close. "I'm gonna have my hands full with you, aren't I?"

I bit my bottom lip with a giggle. "In more ways than one."

"Feed your man, baby."

"Grab a cup of coffee, and I'll get our plates ready," I suggested, stepping away from him to grab a knife.

"How do you take yours?" he asked.

I shouldn't have been surprised that Brodie was making a cup of coffee for me too, without my asking. He'd already shown how considerate he was, but something about the moment's domesticity struck me as so sweet. "A splash of cream and two spoonfuls of sugar, please."

Brodie plowed through everything I made as we sat together and ate. At my look of surprise, he teased, "What? I burned a fuck of a lot of calories making you come."

"That you did," I murmured.

After we finished, he cleaned the kitchen before returning to his surveillance equipment. While he was busy, I got comfy on the couch, using my e-reader to pull up the manuscript for the next book I was going to record. I liked to read through the projects first so I could make notes of any names or words that might trip me up. That way, I could ask for clarification from the author or publisher before heading into the sound booth.

It was the same thing I'd done a hundred times before, in the same spot. But it felt so much better sharing the same space with Brodie even though we weren't doing anything together.

7

ECHO

"I thought you said I had a break," Jeff whined, the irritating sound making me grit my teeth.

"Well, things change, dipshit," growled the voice on the other end of his phone. "The boss found another mark, and you need to get everything set up for your new identity."

This was how they ran their schemes. Jeff was given a new name, bank accounts, apartment, car, etc. Everything that made it appear as if he didn't need money so that the victim would trust him more easily.

Wizard had been impressed with their thoroughness. It would take someone with considerable skill to tear through the walls they'd built around the fake persona.

"I emailed you the documents," the man informed Jeff. "But you need to pick up the rest of it tomorrow at noon."

Jeff sighed dramatically, and I could picture him pouting like a spoiled little kid.

Such an asshole.

"Where?" he asked.

"The coffee shop by the library. Don't be late."

"Yeah, whatever," Jeff huffed, then the line went silent, telling me that he'd hung up.

I wrote down the information on a notepad, as I listened to him move around then heard the sound of his front door shutting. Since he was gone, I removed my headphones and grabbed my cell to call Wizard, who picked up after the first ring.

"You get it?" I questioned.

"Too many relays," he replied with a frustrated grunt. "These fuckers aren't messing around. Whoever is in charge has deep pockets."

"Dammit," I muttered, running a hand through my hair. "We'll have to put a tail on both of them after their meeting."

"Already on it. Sent a text to Prez, and he's sending Ink and Shadow to go with you. Kevlar and Cross are comin' to guard your woman."

I nodded even though he couldn't see it. "Great."

Both men were club enforcers and knew how to stay out of sight. Shadow had picked up his skills as a former thief, but Ink had ties to the southern mafia, and they'd given him many skills that came in very handy.

"Tell Ink and Shadow to meet me at the library at eleven thirty."

"Got it."

After ending the call, I noticed Violet standing a couple of feet away, craning her neck to look at my surveillance equipment. She seemed fascinated, and a smile spread across my face.

Holding out my hand, I motioned her toward me. "C'mere, baby."

She hurried to close the distance between us, and I pulled her onto my lap, then gave her a quick tutorial of the setup. When my phone buzzed, she glanced at it with disappointment, and I chuckled.

"Go ahead and try it out," I told her as I helped her to her feet. "I'll just be a few minutes."

Her face lit up, and my smile grew. She was so fucking cute.

I walked out onto her balcony and saw the name of the club's treasurer, Ace, flashing on the screen. He was brilliant with money and kept our accounts more than flush. However, he'd been given his road name because of his gambling. It wasn't an addiction, though —he wasn't reckless. But he rarely lost and had cleaned out several patches while he'd been a prospect.

"What's up?" I greeted when I'd answered the call.

"Wizard sent me some more financials to do some forensic accounting. Think I finally found a new lead."

I'd have been happy to hear the news a couple of days ago, but now that I'd met and claimed Violet, I was fucking thrilled because I was itching to get this shit handled as fast as possible.

"Go on."

"I don't think women are the only targets for this group," he announced, astounding me.

"You've got to be shitting me," I muttered.

"Been looking for similar spending patterns near Jeff's last half dozen victims and ran into a couple that were strikingly similar."

Jeff had an arsenal of "moves" when running a con, and it had made it easier for us to narrow down the woman he was fleecing by following his money transactions. Wizard had found them by combing through security footage, reservations that required an ID for both participants, and even shit like flower deliveries.

"Except in these two cases, there was a significant age gap between the man and woman—at least twenty years—but the woman disappeared in the end, taking everything valuable and leaving an empty bank account."

"Okay," I agreed. He'd convinced me, but I still didn't see how this helped us get closer to the boss. "There a connection between either of the women and Jeff?"

"Not yet. Just wanted to fill you in so you can be on the lookout for anything that might help with that avenue as well."

"Noted. Let me know if you find anything else."

"Sure, brother."

I chewed on the information from Ace for a few minutes before going back inside. Violet was still tinkering with my equipment, but she glanced up at me with a beautiful smile when she heard me walk in and slide the glass door closed.

Her cheeks turned pink, and she giggled. "I don't know how any of this would help with my job, but it's so cool. I'm trying to come up with an excuse."

I gestured to the setup and winked at her. "If I'm not using it, it's yours to play with."

She double blinked, and her deep purple eyes danced with delight. "Really?"

I grinned and walked over to stand in front of her. She'd taken my seat, so I bent over and gripped the arms of the chair, caging her in. "What's mine is yours, baby."

Her smile turned sly, and she quipped, "Does that include your body?"

My lips brushed across hers, then slid along her jaw until I reached her ear. "*Especially* my body."

She shivered, and I groaned, pissed at Jeff for a whole other reason now. "Gonna have to wait until I get back, though," I informed her reluctantly.

"You have to leave?" Her bottom lip popped out just a little in an adorable pout. I took it between my teeth and tugged, before letting go and smacking a hard kiss on her mouth.

"Got to check on something. But a couple of prospects will be downstairs by the front and back doors of the building. Our sergeant at arms, Kevlar, and captain, Cross, will be across the hall in the apartment I was using before. They'll be listening, so if you're scared or need anything, just call out to them."

Violet nodded, chewing on her lip as she stared up at me. "Just be careful," she whispered finally.

I replied by giving her a deep kiss, then murmured against her lips, "Don't be doing anything that will have you making those sexy sounds I love to hear when I fuck you. Or I'll have to kill them." Her eyes widened, and my gaze swept down her delicious curves. "Hmmm. I'm making that a permanent rule, baby. Only I get to make you come, is that understood?"

Violet hummed her agreement, her purple orbs cloudy with desire.

It was hard as fuck—no pun intended—to leave her with that soft look and ripe body there for the taking. But I wanted this shit over with so we could move on with our lives. Hopefully, by the time her property patch was complete, she'd have my ring on her finger and my baby in her belly.

Shadow and Ink were waiting when I pulled into the parking lot on my motorcycle. I'd driven the Jeep to Violet's that first night, but a couple of the guys had brought my bike over the next day.

I hadn't had a chance to take Violet out on it, but I was itching to feel her wrapped around me with the wind in my face and my engine hummed beneath us. Just the thought of the ride had me hard as steel, but I was gonna take her to a spot I'd discovered. One that was isolated and would give us the perfect cover for me to fuck her on the back of my motorcycle.

Shaking my head, I pushed those images away before I exploded in my jeans like a horny teenager.

"Echo," Shadow greeted me as I swung my leg over the seat and dismounted.

I nodded to them both as I shrugged out of my cut and stowed it in my saddle bag, then put on a leather jacket.

"Those for us?" I asked, lifting my chin toward three dark, nondescript sedans.

"Yeah," Ink confirmed. He and Shadow had both removed their cuts as well. We didn't want to draw attention to the MC if spotted. Ink—who was an incredible artist and tattooist, with a huge waiting list at our tattoo parlor, Hellbound Studio—had also donned a buttoned up, long-sleeved Henley in order to cover a good portion of the designs that covered his body. "Jeff isn't here yet, but only two guys are in the café. One of them looks like he's packing heat. Unsure if the other is with him or not."

"Keep it simple," I instructed as I checked over my weapon before shoving it into the back of my pants so the piece was fully hidden by my jacket. "Ink, I want you on Jeff. Shadow and I will tail the contact unless it looks like they're both involved, then we'll split up."

Both men nodded, and then we got settled inside the cars, the three of us still linked through earpieces Wizard had specifically designed for the club.

"On approach," Ink muttered, and I glanced at the small parking lot by the coffee house, seeing Jeff pulling in. I'd obviously bugged his car and tapped his phone, but we needed to monitor all his communication, including in-person conversations. So Wizard and I had created a small device to cling to his hair near his scalp with a micro silicone link ring bead. He couldn't see or feel it, it wasn't affected by water or soap, and a comb wouldn't dislodge it. I'd slipped him a pill on my first night in the building so I could break in and attach the bug.

"Sully," Jeff greeted the bigger of the two men as he approached the table.

Sully grunted in response and shoved a folder at Jeff when he sat down. "Did you look through the information I sent?"

Jeff sighed—he did that often, and it was annoying as fuck. How he managed to swindle women was beyond me.

"Give me a break," he snapped. "You only sent it a couple of hours ago. I always know my shit when the job starts, so stop treating me like this is my first one."

If I hadn't been watching all of the men so carefully, I might have missed the subtle cue from the third guy when Jeff's tone became belligerent.

"Looks like we're each on our own," Shadow muttered in my ear.

Sully glared at Jeff as he continued talking. "This mark is practically on death's door. That's why Gene is cutting your break short. The woman's been talking about completing her bucket list. That's where the rugged, down-to-earth construction worker comes in."

I scoffed, wondering how the fuck they expected Jeff to pull that off, then my jaw dropped as I watched him morph into someone else entirely.

Gone was the spoiled, perverted, sniveling little bitch. In his place was a confident man with a hard edge but kind eyes. Even wearing the preppy shit he had on, he looked tougher and rough around the edges.

"Damn."

"Holy shit," Ink hissed.

"And the Oscar goes to..." Shadow murmured in an amused tone.

A growl rumbled in Jeff's chest as he scowled at

Sully and picked up the folder. When he held out his hand, Sully dropped a set of keys onto his palm.

"For the apartment, the 'construction office'"—he used air quotes to indicate that it was fake—"and a fob for a new Ford F-150 Lightning. You're scheduled to fix a leaky window on Monday at ten in the morning."

Jeff nodded and stood from the table, and like it had a few minutes before, a transformation took over his body. The irritating, juvenile motherfucker was back. He glanced over at the other guy for just a second, then mumbled to Sully, "Tell Gene I'm tired of the middlemen. I do one-on-one with the boss, or I walk."

Sully's eyes narrowed, but he didn't otherwise react. After a beat, Jeff pivoted on his heel and marched out of the café.

"Think that's Gene?" Ink asked, referring to the other man in the coffee house.

"Doesn't look like a shot caller to me," Shadow mused.

I grunted an agreement as I watched Jeff approach his vehicle. When he opened the door, I ordered, "Go."

I knew my boys would be all over their assignments, so I focused solely on my target. Sully didn't give the other patron even a single side glance as he got up from the table and lumbered outside. He watched Jeff drive away with his face twisted into a sneer.

He was in his car and turning onto the main road when my cell beeped in my ear. Easing out of the parking lot, I kept a safe distance from Sully and pressed the button on my earbud to answer the call.

Ace didn't wait for me to give him a greeting. "Know you're tailing the suspect, but I have some info I thought you should know."

"I need to know it now?" I grumped.

"Could change what you're looking for."

"Fine. Go ahead."

Sully drove like an old woman anyway, making it easier for me to listen to Ace.

"After untangling some of the mess of shell companies for a few of Jeff's accounts, I noticed that some of the deposits made into them originated from businesses unlikely to be owned by men."

"You know this because…?"

"Would you name your company 'Twilight Technologies'? Or 'Charming Capital Co'? Or my personal favorite, 'The Glam Group'."

"I see your point," I conceded. "Not solid proof, though. The boss's name is Gene."

"True, but those companies were also the original source of deposits made into two accounts besides Jeff's. The owners fit the description I gave you earlier today. Young, beautiful, and dating much older men."

"Sounds like you're right about the targets, but I still don't understand why it matters that some of the shell companies might be registered to women. Gene must have other people on the payroll. Could be he used one of them to set up the companies."

"Maybe, but from everything we've learned, it doesn't sound like this guy is much for delegating or giving up even the slightest bit of control."

Sully slowed in front of a spectacular mansion and turned into the circle drive.

"Hold up," I told Ace before he could reply.

I sped up a little and stopped at the next intersection so I could flip a U-turn, then pulled to a stop on the shoulder of the road across from the mansion.

"Just wait a second. He's going inside a house, and I need to set up my parabolic mic so I can hear what's going on in there."

Ace remained silent while I went to work. It only took a minute to have it ready to go, and when I turned it on, Sully seemed to be just arriving.

"Gene," he greeted from somewhere on the second floor. "It's done."

There was movement at one of the floor-to-ceiling windows upstairs, and I grabbed my binoculars, directing them to that spot.

The curtain slid away from the window, and shock blew through my system when the boss replied, "Good."

"Motherfucker," I sputtered—something I'd only ever done once before...the moment I first saw Violet.

"Everything okay?" Ace queried, his tone alert.

"Yeah. I'm just...fucking hell. I'm looking at the boss, and I think we got the name wrong."

"Gene isn't in charge?" Ace asked, his voice filled with frustration.

"Uh, no. That's the boss. Only, I'm guessing her name is spelled J-E-A-N instead of G-E-N-E."

"Her? No fucking way."

"Yup. The ringleader is a fucking woman."

8

VIOLET

Brodie had let me get a good look at his audio surveillance equipment this morning while he was on the phone with someone from his club, so when he got home later that afternoon, I figured I'd return the favor.

"My stuff isn't as cool as yours, but this is where the magic happens," I said, cringing at how cheesy that sounded. I was proud of what I'd accomplished in here—from how I'd hung each soundproofing square and blanket myself to all the audiobooks I'd recorded.

My vocal booth was larger than most, but I liked having the extra space while recording so that I didn't feel penned in. I'd even put up a few strings of fairy lights to give the space a fun spin, which also helped make the recording sessions I streamed live a little less boring.

The only furniture in the room was my large desk. Brodie headed straight for it to take a closer look at the double monitors and microphone perched on top of the flat surface. His feet didn't even make a sound on the carpet as he moved across the floor, his blue eyes darting in every direction as if he was examining every inch he passed.

"The reading I did curled up on the couch was really prep work," I explained, taking a seat on my large, comfy desk chair. I turned on my computer and tapped on the keyboard to pull up the notes I'd sent to myself from my e-reader. "Now I know what to ask the author before I start recording."

"Have you tested how soundproof the room actually is?" he asked, swiveling my chair to face him.

"I mean, my neighbors haven't complained so far," I replied with a laugh, but it was quickly cut short when he leaned over, his lips trailing my neck. "But you were able to listen in while I was recording."

"Only because I microphoned the fuck out of the area surrounding Jeff's apartment, and I still had to crank up the volume and filter out a fuck ton of background noise." His breath was hot against my skin, and I sighed, leaning into his touch. "No matter how loud you get, your neighbors aren't gonna hear you as long as we're in here."

"You think so?" I whispered, my breath hitching when he nipped at my pulse point.

"I know so, baby, or else I wouldn't be planning for all the ways I'm about to make you scream my name as loud as you can," he rasped. "No way in fuck do I want anyone else to know how you sound when you fall apart for me."

He bent over to capture my mouth in a deep kiss, leaving me in a sensual fog when he quickly turned my chair back around to face the desk again. Standing behind me, I couldn't see Brodie's movements as his lips trailed down my neck while his hands went under the thin material of my shirt. I shivered when his fingers trailed over my sensitive skin until he reached my silky bra.

My nipples peaked at his touch, and I arched my back to press my breasts deeper into his hands. "The things I want to do to these perfect tits should be illegal."

"Like what?" All sorts of filthy fantasies flashed through my brain, inspired by my reading.

His hands shifted so he was cupping my breasts. Then he pressed them close together, making the valley between them more pronounced. "Sometime soon, I'm gonna shove my hard cock between these beauties and watch you wrap your sweet lips around the head each time I thrust up."

That sounded like something I wanted to experience. Immediately. "Soon? Not today?"

"My good girl wants to be bad for me?" he asked, swiveling my chair again so that he could yank my shirt up and nibble along the strap of my bra.

I squeezed my thighs together to ease the ache between them. "I really, really do."

"Then get as loud as you can while I make you come, baby." He gently tugged my pebbled nipple with his teeth before letting go with a pop, leaving a wet spot on the silky material that cupped my rounded globe. "I want to feel your pussy walls clenched around my cock when I come, and that's not gonna happen if I live out that particular fantasy right now. You're too fucking sexy for me to last long enough to get inside you."

I felt a feminine thrill at his words, loving how Brodie didn't hesitate to let me know exactly how sexy he found me. It was a rush to know that I had so much power over him.

He peeled off my shirt, dropping it to the floor before pushing my bra cups down, my already hardened nipples now at full attention as his tongue made its way along my neck and collarbone.

I cried out when he sucked one into his mouth, my hips shooting forward as though an electric jolt had gone straight to my core.

Brodie chuckled. "Don't hold back, baby. You can be as loud as you want while we're in here."

Before I had a chance to think of a response, another electric zing shot through me as he blew his warm breath over my nipple before sucking hard on the bud. Moaning, I let my eyes flutter closed as I leaned back into the chair.

I was so wrapped up in the pleasure he was giving me that I didn't notice that he'd moved. But when his mouth left my nipple, I let out a little whimper of protest and opened my eyes to find him kneeling between my legs.

He didn't say anything as he removed my bra, leggings, and panties, leaving me completely bare for him. But his eyes stayed on mine as he dipped down, kissing the inside of my thighs before blowing a hot blast of air over my pussy.

"Brodie," I moaned, widening my legs a little more to give him better access.

"That's right, my good girl," he praised. "Use

that sexy voice of yours to let me know how much you like what I'm doing to you."

Goose bumps prickled at his sensual demand, one I couldn't deny. Thrusting my fingers into his thick hair, I pulled his face closer to me as I cried, "More please, Brodie."

"You want this?" he asked, blowing another hot breath, his gaze locked on mine. "Or do you need more to make you scream? To have you testing the soundproofing you put up on these walls until they shake while you come hard on my face, calling out my name?"

I swallowed hard. That was exactly what I wanted, but it was a lot harder to say the words when it was what I wanted in real life, not a script I was reading from. Getting what I needed was worth the effort, though, so I forced my lips to move. "I need more, please."

He grinned, finally running his tongue down my slit. "Good girl."

I didn't have a chance to react to that statement because his mouth started to devour my pussy with long licks between my lower lips before he sucked my clit so hard that I saw stars. My hips bucked toward his face as though they had a mind of their own.

He moaned into my sensitive flesh, adding a hooked finger that he swirled along my walls while still sucking my clit. I gripped the chair so hard that my knuckles turned white, my whole body on fire.

The heat started low in my belly before it exploded through me. I didn't hold back as I rode out my orgasm on his face, yelling, "Yes! Oh, Brodie! Yes!"

He licked up every last drop of my release, moaning as he did so. But he didn't stop when he was done. Instead, he increased the pace of his finger and added another, twirling it inside me as his magic tongue and lips worked on my clit.

It didn't take long for another orgasm to hit, and I saw stars, feeling them through every part of my body as I cried out his name again before slumping back on the chair. Aftershocks tore through me, all it took was for Brodie to kiss my thighs to make me moan again. "Whoa."

Before I knew what was happening, he had his arms around my waist and lifted me into the air.

"What are you doing?" I squealed as he walked through the room, pushing the blanket aside from the door.

"Figured you'd be too tired to walk. I'm putting

my cock in you for only the second time. I want it to be on the bed," he murmured.

When he laid me on the mattress, I looked up at him with a pout. "But you're still dressed."

"Not for long." He quickly stripped out of his clothes.

The man had abs for days, and a full sleeve of black ink. His dick was truly impressive, leaking at the tip, but it was the small hoop through his right nipple that caught my eye.

I grinned, leaning forward and taking the silver circle in my teeth and sucking his nipple along with it.

A deep groan rumbled up his chest, but he put his hands on my shoulders to gently push me back. "As much as I want you to keep doing that, I'm on a hair trigger here, baby. I need to get inside you before I come."

I sucked in a breath at his words and leaned back, spreading myself for him, beyond ready to feel him inside me. His blue eyes burned with need as he kneeled on the bed and slowly slid his dick inside me, letting me adjust to his girth. Once he filled me to the hilt, I let out a sigh of pleasure.

"Love how fucking wet you are for me."

He circled his hips, and my inner walls clenched around his dick.

"That's it, baby. Choke my cock, take it all." He punctuated his command with a hard thrust.

Each movement felt better than the last, my whole body on fire as I moaned, letting the pleasure take over. "Yessssss! I'm so close, Brodie."

"Then come for me, Violet. Now," he growled, pushing harder before sliding his hand between us, massaging my clit in the same motion his dick pumped in and out of me.

It didn't take long for me to explode, crying out his name as my body shook from the orgasm.

He followed suit quickly after, filling me completely as he kissed me long and slow, his body still attached to mine as he pumped out the last of his release. Without a condom. Something we hadn't really talked about yet, but I knew we should. When I wasn't completely drained from mind-blowing orgasms and could think more clearly.

9

ECHO

Once we realized that the person in charge of the con ring was a woman, Wizard had a fuck of a lot more to work with. So he told us to give him twenty-four hours to put together everything he could find with all the information he'd already gathered.

We had eyes on the two women in the middle of a scheme and on Jeff, who hadn't initiated his next job yet. If necessary, we'd interfere to keep the marks from being taken advantage of before we could take down Jean and her lackeys.

After Violet and I had our little romp in her recording studio—followed by her bed, the floor, and finally, the shower—I made her dinner. Then we relaxed on the couch with a movie while we ate.

She'd seemed delighted that I'd cooked for her, but it was nothing compared to how elated I was when she pulled a chocolate melting cake from the oven. By the time we'd finished the whole thing, she had a new appreciation for the gooey center since I'd eaten most of it on her pussy.

I asked King to keep Ink on Jeff so I could have some uninterrupted time with my woman while we waited on Wizard and Ace to find our smoking gun.

Not having to worry about surveillance meant I could focus solely on Violet. The result was that she was gonna be sore as hell after I fucked her relentlessly. I couldn't get enough of her...or fucking her bare. I knew we should have talked about it, but the feeling of her tight pussy wrapped around my naked cock was pure heaven. And it didn't completely slip my mind that every time I came inside her, it was one more shot at knocking her up.

"Damn," I grunted the following morning as we lay sprawled out in the bed, both of us spent from our last round of sexual acrobatics.

"Uh-huh," Violet panted, her body draped over mine with my semi-hard cock still sheathed in her hot center.

She shifted, and her inner muscles clenched, making me groan and grab her hips to keep her still.

"You gotta stop that, baby," I warned. "Or you won't be able to walk tomorrow."

Violet giggled and turned her face into my chest, placing a soft kiss on my nipple ring, then laying her cheek on my pec. "If anyone had said that to me a few days ago, I would have thought they were crazy."

"And now?" I pressed, grinning down at her.

She shrugged and turned her head to look up at me, resting her chin on my torso. "It doesn't sound all that unappealing."

"Motherfucker," I rasped, silently shouting at my cock to stand down.

It didn't give a shit what my brain wanted. A burst of energy filled me, and I flipped us over, put Violet's legs on my shoulders, and pounded in and out of her vise-like pussy. When her cries escalated, I pressed a hand over her mouth to muffle her screams.

When this shit was over, the first thing I was gonna do was find us a house that was isolated enough that she could shout the walls down, and no one would hear her.

After we both found fulfillment, we collapsed again and fell into an exhausted sleep. We only slept for a little over an hour, then we snuggled in bed and talked for a while. When she fell silent for a little too long, I put two fingers under her chin and raised her head so I could clearly see her face.

"What's on your mind, baby?"

She watched me hesitantly for a moment before speaking. "I know you can't tell me everything, but... can you share anything? Did you accomplish what you needed to yesterday?"

I sighed and leaned back on my pillow, studying the ceiling as I contemplated how much to share. "We found Jeff's boss. Just going to take a little time to put things into place so we can take the group down completely."

"Oh."

She sounded so dejected that I rolled us over so I could study her expression when I asked, "What's that tone for?"

Violet licked her lips and glanced away.

"Look at me, Violet," I ordered.

Her purple gaze returned to my face, and we locked eyes.

"So you don't need my apartment anymore?" she queried softly. "Since you don't need Jeff to lead you to the guy in charge?"

I immediately understood her change in demeanor, and smug satisfaction bloomed in my chest. "You think we're done because I found another lead to follow?"

She nodded, and her violet pools glistened with tears, even though she was blinking rapidly to hold them back.

"Think again, baby," I growled. "This"—I pointed back and forth between us—"will never be done."

Hope sparked in her beautiful eyes, and her chest froze as if she was holding her breath.

"I meant it when I said you were mine, baby. There's no going back now."

Her mouth widened into a brilliant smile, and she sighed happily. "That's not all that unappealing either."

I raised an eyebrow and narrowed my eyes. "Just not unappealing? Clearly, I haven't been doing my job."

By the time I let her out of bed, she agreed that being mine was the best idea ever as she wobbled to the bathroom on unsteady legs.

We spent the day together, working on our shit between christening every room and piece of sturdy furniture in her apartment.

She let me listen while she recorded the first chapter of her newest project, and I completely understood why she was so sought after. I'd been caught up in the story, transported there by her voice and the way she weaved her words. It was magic.

When we went to bed that night, we were both so damn tired that we slept like the dead. I'd just plated our breakfast and placed it in front of Violet at the bar when my phone rang from the bedroom.

"Be right back, baby," I told her, giving her a quick kiss before stalking to the other room.

It was Blaze calling so I quickly answered. "Yeah?"

"Hope I'm not interrupting," he chortled.

"Wouldn't have answered the damn phone, asshole," I grumbled.

"Fair enough. Wizard's got something. Get your ass to the clubhouse."

"Violet's eating breakfast. As soon as she's done, we'll head over."

"Fine. Also, I ordered the vest. Should be here next week."

"Thanks."

"Don't mention it."

I ended the call as I returned to the kitchen and put my arms around my woman, burying my face in the crook of her neck. Damn, she smelled amazing.

"Gotta go to the clubhouse for some business," I told her. "I want you to come with me."

She twisted her neck, and I raised my head to gauge her expression. She looked stunned but pleased, making me grin. "You want to take me to the Hounds of Hellfire clubhouse?"

I nodded. "You'll be safest there. And I want you with me."

"But isn't that like...secret or something?"

Laughing, I kissed her nose and shook my head. "It's not exactly secret. More like...exclusive."

"But I thought only club bunnies and old ladies got to be in the clubhouse."

I rolled my eyes and scooped her into my arms. "You've been reading too many of those novels, baby. First, there are no 'club bunnies' around our MC. Not since several years before King took over as our prez. And Stella would kick all our asses if someone even tried to suggest it."

Violet giggled as I bounced her a little while strolling back to the bedroom and into the master bath. She didn't bring up the second half of her statement again, and without a property patch to give her, I left that subject alone for the moment.

We showered and dressed, then scarfed down

our now cold breakfast before hopping on my bike and riding to the compound.

Blaze stood by the hallway that led to the offices when we walked inside, talking quietly with Ace and Ink. He stopped when he spotted me and jerked his chin, a silent order to follow him.

I nodded, then turned to Violet and walked her over to one of the couches in the lounge. "Got club business to deal with. You want me to take you to my room so you can lie down or read?"

She smiled and shook her head, dropping onto the couch. "Nope. I'm good here." She put her feet up and fished her e-reader out of her purse, then shot me a content smile. "Take your time."

The sincerity in her voice astonished me. How had I met the perfect fucking woman for me? I didn't deserve Violet, that was for sure. But nothing would stop me from keeping her.

It was on the tip of my tongue to tell her I loved her, but it was definitely not the right time. Instead, I stalked over to her and gave her a hard, hot kiss before heading to King's office.

King, Blaze, Wizard, Ace, Ink, Shadow, Kevlar, and Cross were all at the conference table to the right of the door. I grabbed one of the other chairs and sat, halting their hushed conversation.

"Wizard?" King prompted.

Wizard pushed a folder in each of our directions, then leaned back in his chair and tapped the keyboard of his laptop, which was perched on the table in front of him. "That's pretty much everything we know about this group. There's also a chart for the hierarchy and an info sheet on each of the key players."

He continued to share what he'd learned, with Ace jumping in from time to time. Idea after idea on how to finish things swirled around in my head, and from the thoughtful expressions on everyone's faces, I had a feeling they were similarly occupied.

Finally, Wizard ran out of steam, and the questions started. We tossed out suggestions, analyzed some of the data more thoroughly, and worked the problem from every angle to find a solution.

"Hold up," Shadow murmured, staring at one of the sheets of paper in his hand. "Jean has been married six times?"

Wizard nodded. "Younger men. No prenup."

"She was already filthy rich when she started this shit?" Kevlar blurted, tossing his folder on the table with a disgusted huff.

"Yup."

"She does it for the thrill, then," Shadow surmised.

"Fair assumption," King agreed, his gaze locked on Shadow. "You think it would work?"

"Would what work?" Ink asked, his eyes darting back and forth between the two of them.

"Maybe," I grunted, catching on to their train of thought once I digested Shadow's words. "Only if there is a compelling reason for her to get back in the game."

"The fuck are you three *not* talking about?" snapped Blaze.

Shadow scratched his chin, then set down his folder and tapped his finger on it. "If we want to take down the entire organization, we have to get Jean. Not just the underlings because she'll just hire new ones."

"We need to catch her in a con," I added.

"Exactly."

King folded his arms over his chest and leaned back against his chair. "How do we get her back in the game?"

"Bait," Cross tossed out. "A fish so big and illusive that she can't help herself."

I sat back and propped an ankle on the opposite knee. "Appeal to her ego and her love of the thrill," I mused.

Ace rapped his knuckles on the table twice, then snatched Wizard's laptop.

"What the hell?!" Wizard bellowed, his face a mask of outrage.

The rest of us stared at Ace, absolutely dumbfounded. Taking Wizard's computer was the fastest way to change your address to the nearest cemetery.

"Chill the fuck out, man," Ace said distractedly as he quickly typed. "Not like I stole your kidney or something."

Wizard's face turned purple as he seethed, glaring daggers at Ace while curling his hands into fists so tight his knuckles cracked.

I shot a look at King, wondering if he'd step in, but he was watching the two of them with amusement, something we rarely saw from the prez unless he was with his old lady or son.

"You gonna save his ass?" I asked Blaze quietly, who was sitting next to me.

"Nah. Fifty says Ace ends up in the hospital tonight."

There were several murmured agreements, making King chuckle.

"You have a death wish, Ace?" Cross murmured,

watching Wizard warily from the treasurer's left side.

He grunted and tapped hard on one key, then slid the laptop back over in front of Wizard.

Taking a deep breath, Wizard tore his eyes from his prey to scan the computer screen. "This is good," he admitted grudgingly. "Not gonna save you from being stabbed in your sleep when you're least expecting it, though."

Ace rolled his eyes. "It will if you want my help with the financial shit."

Wizard ground his teeth, but he didn't say anything else.

"You two done?" King grunted, his face back in its usual scowl.

Ace gestured to the computer and explained, "Wizard and I have the beginnings of several aliases set up for cases when we need to get someone gone fast. One of them is for a high roller. Someone who wants to disappear with their fortune and can afford to pay us to do it since it takes a fuck ton of work."

Wizard nodded. "Won't take much work to get this up and running. The back end is as solid as they get. Breaking this identity would take years for the best of the best. Once it's live, we filter word of the new man through the grapevine, and as long as we're reading her right, she'll bite."

"Volunteers?" Ace asked with a smirk.

I sighed. "It's my op, I'll do it."

Blaze and King shared a look, then they both grinned and King suggested, "Bring Violet in here to tell her."

"Why?" I questioned, my eyes narrowed in suspicion.

"Protection," Blaze drawled.

I scowled. "Why would Violet need protection?"

"Not Violet, Echo," King muttered as he stood and walked around his desk to take a seat behind it. "You."

"What?"

Blaze swept his hand around the table and grunted. "Out."

They all protested but shut up and left when King growled. "Now!"

Ace was the last to reach the door. "I'll send in your woman," he told me before leaving.

I was pacing in front of King's desk, much to Blaze's amusement, when Violet stepped into the room.

"Hi," she said softly, giving the prez and VP respectful nods. Then she came directly to my side, and I curled my arm around her waist before giving her a soft kiss.

"Hey, baby."

"Is everything okay?"

"Yeah. King gave me permission to bring you further into the loop on some of this shit with the con organization."

"Oh?" Her eyebrows shot up into her hair, and her mouth formed a cute little O.

"Let's sit," I prompted, guiding her over to the couch. Once I settled, I tugged her onto my lap. "You know Jeff is a low-level conman. And I told you we were going after the big fish."

"Yes," she agreed with a nod.

"Well, we discovered the other day—when I had to leave for a few hours—that the boss is actually a woman."

"No way!" Violet gasped. "Seriously?"

I went on to explain more about her and our plan to take her down. When I got to the bait part, her expression fell, then darkened as I continued, and by the time I finished, she looked absolutely livid.

"Are you kidding me, Brodie Fauks?" she shouted, jumping to her feet.

I heard a deep chuckle and tossed a glare at Blaze, who was grinning behind Violet's back.

"Shouldn't take long," I assured her. "I'll play the part of the mark, give her what she wants until we catch her trying to steal the money from the dummy account we set up. You'll stay here in the clubhouse where you're protected."

"You're going to give her what she wants?" Violet asked in an emotionless tone.

"You are so fucked, brother," King muttered as he shook his head.

"For shit's sake," I barked. "It's not like I'll actually be dating the woman!"

Violet inhaled slowly and crossed her arms under her breasts, pushing them up and distracting me with thoughts of how they tasted and what they'd feel like wrapped around my—

"Focus, Brodie!" Violet stomped her foot and growled, forcing me to mash my lips together so I wouldn't smile at how damn cute she was.

I locked my eyes with her gorgeous purple orbs and tried not to think about how fucking bad I needed to be inside her.

"Let's look at this from another perspective, shall we?" she asked in an overly sweet tone that put me on edge. The smirks on King's and Blaze's faces didn't help either.

"Let's say that the mastermind of this group was

an older man. A man who had a preference for much younger women. Particularly curvy girls with brown hair who were of average height."

"Don't forget violet eyes," Blaze piped up. "He likes those, too."

I glared at my VP for a moment before turning my attention back to my woman.

"And let's assume that in order to put this man in jail, someone needs to pretend to date him. Oh, for the sake of ease, let's say me. I'm the bait, so I have to let him think he has rights to me, to let him take me out, show me off, give me jewels and dresses, and tell me what to wear. Possibly even try to steal a kiss—"

"No!" I bellowed, jumping to my feet. "Not a fucking chance in hell, Violet!"

"Exactly," she huffed, a triumphant smile curling her lips.

"Walked right into that one," King rumbled.

"Fine," I gritted out through clenched teeth. "Get one of the other guys to do it."

Blaze snickered until I turned my lethal gaze on him. "Think Courtney would let you be the one? I'll go tell her you volunteered."

That shut him up real fucking quick.

"Brodie, don't be mean," Violet chastised, her voice back to its normal sweet and sultry tone.

I held out my hand. "Let's go," I rasped, desperate to be alone with her.

"Is this Violet?" an excited female voice squealed. "I've been so excited to meet you!"

Knowing King would put a bullet in my head if I looked at Stella with anything less than a pleasant expression, I schooled my face and turned to greet her.

"Hey, Stella. This is my Violet."

Some of the frenzy inside me began to settle when my girl looked up at me with a bright smile and pink cheeks, her dimples on full display. Damn, she was beautiful.

"Come on, we're dying to get to know you," Stella uttered as she grabbed Violet's hand and dragged her from the room.

"I'm gonna give her a tour first," I said loudly as I caught up to them. "We'll meet you back in the lounge in an hour."

Stella pouted, but King gave me a knowing look as he slipped his arm around his wife and guided her away. "I'm sure she'll want to meet Cadell, baby. Let's see if he's up from his nap."

Before anything else could get in my way, I tossed Violet over my shoulder and practically ran to my room.

10

VIOLET

When Brodie brought me to the Hounds of Hellfire compound, I had expected everything I'd ever learned in romance books about motorcycle clubs to be proved wrong. But the clubhouse looked pretty close to what I'd pictured, and his president and VP seemed to be just as in love with their wives as my favorite book boyfriends were with their old ladies.

After I nixed their whole bait idea, Brodie gave me a full tour, although we spent most of it in his room where he repeatedly made me tell him who I belonged to before letting me come. Then we hung out in the lounge with some of his club brothers, Stella, and Courtney.

"How did you two meet?" Stella asked as she

settled her baby boy against her chest to gently pat his back, soothing his little whimpers of complaint.

The pretty blonde wore a black leather vest over her outfit that proclaimed her as belonging to King, the Hounds of Hellfire prez. A property patch, just like the heroines in the fictional clubs I'd read about.

"I live next door to a guy Brodie is looking into," I explained.

"Brodie, huh?" Courtney teased, quirking a brow.

He didn't seem the least bit bothered by it as he slid his hand across my shoulder to wrap his palm around the back of my neck. I was seated on the end of a long couch, with him perched on the arm next to me. I leaned deeper into his side and curved my lips into a pleased smile. I knew what point the VP's wife was making—Brodie would never have had me use anything but his road name if I wasn't special to him.

"Yup," he muttered. "Knew I had to find a way to bump into Violet just from her voice. If her neighbor wasn't such an asshole, I'd owe him a debt of gratitude."

My cheeks heated as I remembered the scene he'd heard me narrate and thanked my lucky stars that his friends had no idea what he was talking about.

"Stalker much?" Courtney asked with a giggle, making Blaze shake his head with a sigh.

Brodie shrugged. "A guy's gotta do what he's gotta do to get his woman's attention."

"Damn straight," King agreed, cupping the back of his son's head with a soft smile that had Stella blushing.

"I'm sure some light stalking wouldn't scare Violet off after she narrated that book for Thea Drummond with the hero who took his masked stalker rep very seriously."

The room went silent as we all turned to gawk at Wizard. I didn't know much about Brodie's club brother, but I never expected him to know the hook line for one of Thea's books even though it was listed on the cover. Or to know the author's real surname and not just the shortened version she used for her pen name.

My eyes were wide as I asked, "You're familiar with *The Monster Behind the Mask*?"

"Stumbled across it when I was looking into you."

"Looking into me?" I echoed, turning to glare at Brodie. "So you knew a lot more about me than just that I was an audiobook narrator when you rescued me from Jeff that day?"

"Not much," he insisted with an unrepentant grin. "Didn't read the report too closely."

"Really?" I asked, my brows drawn together.

Brodie traced his finger over my lips, nodding. "Once I saw your picture, I fell even harder for your face than your voice."

"Awww," Stella cried, sniffling. "Who knew that Echo had such a way with words?"

"Hey, now. I'm damn good with sweet-talking you, baby," King objected, stroking his thumb across her cheek to capture the tear that spilled out of her eye.

Stella laughed softly. "So good that I had your baby less than a year after we first met."

"Chill, Prez." Wizard shot a wicked smile at Brodie. "At least you don't need to worry about your woman recording sex scenes with another guy."

"What the fuck?" Brodie growled, pushing on my chin to tilt my face toward him. "What exactly does recording sex scenes with another guy entail?"

"Absolutely nothing sexy, that's for sure," I muttered, casting a dirty look Wizard's way as best I could.

"Explain," Brodie demanded.

"Most of the books I've narrated have either been solo or dual narration, where I just record my chapters on my own." I winced, already knowing how much he wouldn't like what I had to say next. "But Thea wanted to give duet narration a try on her next book, which requires more collaboration between her male narrator and me."

"What kind of collaboration?" Brodie asked.

At the same time, Wizard muttered, "He's not *her* male narrator, just the one she hired for the job."

Ignoring his club brother—for now—I focused on the person who mattered to me, Brodie. "Duet narration means that we each handle our character's lines of dialogue, even when the chapter is in the other character's point of view."

"Fuck," Brodie groaned, heaving a deep sigh.

"If it's any consolation, I've only done two other books as a duet and am not a big fan of it." I patted his muscular thigh with an apologetic smile. "If any other author besides Thea asked me to take on this project, I probably would've turned them down. And I don't have more books lined up that require duet narration. I can turn them down in the future, if you prefer."

"I hate to limit your career when you've worked so hard to make a name for yourself, but I gotta admit I'm not a fan of you recording sex scenes with another guy, even if it's just acting and from completely different rooms."

I didn't miss how some of the tension in his shoulders eased at my offer. And if I was being completely honest with myself, I got a feminine thrill over how possessive Brodie was of me. But that didn't mean I would keep doing something I didn't even enjoy just to push that particular button. "I'm not going to take a hit by turning down duet narration projects. I have a long list of clients who like working with me and get plenty of inquiries from new ones each week. I will need to start slowing down on how many I accept anyway, if I want to have time to spend with you."

"I'll make it worth your while, baby," he vowed before kissing me, not caring that his club brothers were watching.

"Another one bites the dust," Ace joked, elbowing Wizard in the side. Brodie had introduced me to him when we arrived, explaining he was the club's treasurer. With a warning to never play cards against the guy because he was too damn good and didn't mind cheating when necessary. Not that anyone had ever been able to prove it.

Wizard shook his head. "When I claim my woman, I'm not gonna be pussy-whipped enough for her to act out hot-as-fuck sex scenes with another guy."

"Quit starting shit," King rumbled. "I read somewhere that babies are sensitive to their environment. Don't need Cadell to get all worked up."

Wizard raised his hands in a gesture of surrender. "Sorry, Prez."

Cadell let out a soft cry, and everyone's attention turned to the baby. I heaved a sigh of relief to have their focus off Brodie and me.

He dipped his head to my ear and rasped, "You okay?"

I smiled up at him with a nod. "Yeah, I'm still curious about why Thea's books are stuck in Wizard's brain, but I'm having fun."

"There's a reason we go to him when we need intel to be gathered." At my quirked brow, he added, "But I will admit that it's strange since there was no reason for him to dig up anything on the authors you work for beyond their names."

"I'm glad you can see it, too."

I started to glance at Wizard, but my attention was pulled back to Brodie when he added, "And the guy you're doing that duet narration with."

"Are you really going to ask Wizard to look into him?" I asked, my eyes widening.

"After we've wrapped shit up with the ring we're taking down, fuck yeah." His eyes heated. "Gotta make sure he doesn't pose a risk to you, even if your contact with him is limited."

Any irritation I felt over the idea melted away. "I love how you look after me."

"I'm never gonna let anything bad happen to you, Violet," he vowed. "Every inch of you is mine and only mine."

I didn't hesitate to agree. "I am."

"Never had much of anything that I could call all my own, but you gotta know that I take care of what's mine."

11

ECHO

"Why did I let you talk me into this again?" Ash grumbled, yanking on the collar of his tuxedo shirt.

"You have the least ink and went to fucking law school. You can pull off the high class, rich motherfucker better than most of us," I grunted as I watched him on the video monitor from our hotel suite. "Now stop acting like you're uncomfortable in a monkey suit."

"I *am* uncomfortable in a monkey suit," he grumbled. But he quickly dropped his hand and put on a smile when Cynthia—formerly known as Jean—reappeared at his side.

"Hello, darlin'," he drawled, his natural Texan accent thicker than normal.

Ash was the club secretary and our legal counsel. He'd been born with a silver spoon in his mouth, the only child of a Texas politician and his wife, who pretty much had a kid because it polled better. But instead of becoming a spoiled douche, Ash had been an A student and got scholarships to cover his bachelor's and law degree. He'd worked for anything extra that he needed, not taking a single penny from his Mom and Dad.

They played the proud parents, even when he went to work as a public defender, putting a positive spin on it to make themselves look good. Then he went and joined the Hounds of Hellfire and got involved in shady shit that no one could nail us for... because of Ash.

Which put us where we were now. He was playing up his role as the senator's son—who we'd made to look like he'd been a recluse all the years since he dropped out of the media.

It probably made me an asshole, but I laughed hysterically when Ash's parents called, trying to reconnect. Clearly, they'd thought he was returning to their society and wanted to take advantage of the situation or clean it up, depending on his motives. He told them to go fuck themselves.

The best part of having Ash play this role was

that we didn't have to burn one of the aliases that Ace and Wizard had built. We simply had to resurrect Ash's former self. He wasn't happy about it, but he'd agreed, even without King threatening him.

"Elias," she greeted with a beaming smile.

Wizard snorted, and Ash shot a scathing look at the nearest security camera.

I gave Wizard the side-eye and muttered, "Because Baylor Chadwick is so much better than Elias Prescott III?"

Wizard's amusement faded in an instant.

"That's what I thought. Now get your head in the fucking game."

Cynthia put a perfectly manicured hand on Ash's bicep and licked her lips.

I grimaced, feeling relieved that it was Ash and not me out there.

"I just ran into Dev and Hema Pillai. Didn't you go to law school with their son?"

Ash plastered a charming grin on his chiseled face and nodded. "Rishi and I go way back."

"We must get together with him and his wife!" she gasped with a girlish giggle that almost made my ears bleed. "He's running for Congress. I'm sure if you decide to go into politics like your father, Rishi would be a valuable ally."

Cynthia had done her homework before approaching Ash. Luckily, his parents would rather die than admit he was a patch with the Hounds of Hellfire. They'd stuck to any facts that made them look good, building trust in Ash without us having to do a damn thing.

"Are you at all worried that she will try to make him husband number seven instead of her next mark?" Wizard wondered casually.

Ash choked on his champagne, and I swallowed back my laughter when it sent him into a coughing fit. He was gonna kick my ass if I gave him any more reason to. Hopefully, Wizard would keep saying stupid things to get me off the hook.

However, Wizard's concern was valid. Over the past couple of weeks, she'd been making more and more comments about Ash's future in politics and wanting to introduce him to the heads of prestigious law firms. I'd begun to worry about her motives as well. Especially when it had become clear that she was getting frustrated that he hadn't taken her up on her offer to go back to her place or come back to his.

But Ash had been confident that she was still on the con, so we trusted his judgment.

"Are you alright, sweetheart?" Cynthia asked as she rubbed his back in slow circles.

"Sure, darlin'," he croaked with a fake laugh. "I was a little distracted by your beauty, and my drink went down the wrong way."

She batted her lashes at him, and a blush stained her cheeks as she played with the diamond necklace circling her throat.

There was no way that woman had a single thing to blush about.

"I would say I'm sorry, but I can't pretend I'm not flattered."

Ash grinned and slipped his arm around her waist. "It's not flattery if it's true, sweetheart."

"Elias...ummm...would you mind terribly holding this for me?" She held out her small clutch and batted her fake lashes again, and I couldn't help but think that it was weird hearing anyone call him by his full name. The few people who didn't call him by his road name used Eli. "I don't know what I was thinking of bringing that old thing. I completely forgot that the wrist strap was broken."

Ash frowned at the clutch, then gave her a charming smile. "You shouldn't be wearing things that aren't as beautiful as you, darlin'. How about we go shopping tomorrow?"

Cynthia giggled again, making me wince. "Oh,

Elias. You are the sweetest. You don't need to take me shopping!"

"I know I don't need to, sweetheart. I want to. You deserve everything your heart desires. Now, let me take that for you so you don't have to worry about a thing."

She patted her blond updo and blushed before leaning up on her tiptoes to kiss his cheek.

Yeah, Violet had been right to blow a fucking gasket about me being the bait. Any man who put his lips on her was gonna be staring down the barrel of my gun right before they closed their eyes for good. So I couldn't blame her if she'd clawed the woman's eyes out for kissing my cheek.

Ash's eyes came to the camera again, and I saw the desperate plea in them before he managed to shutter it.

"You know what she's after, Ash. Figure out how to give it to her fast, and I'll get you outta there."

"Thank you," she said softly, looping her arm around his. "I realized something this morning as I was picking out my dress."

"Oh? What was that, darlin'?"

"I don't know what your favorite color is!"

Ash laughed and glanced down at her blue silk dress. "Lucky for me, you wore it."

"Say it, Ash," I growled.

"I love blue," he added quickly.

"Really? That's amazing! It's my favorite, too."

"Just keep talking now that you're holding the purse," I instructed him. "As soon as you've given her all the sounds she needs for the voice key, I'll page you for an emergency."

He gave me an almost imperceptible nod, then launched into what was probably the longest conversation he'd ever had. Other than in the courtroom, Ash was a man of few words. But Cynthia needed a passphrase recorded in Ash's voice to get into his servers. She had a tech guy on the payroll, and he'd told her all she needed was the specific sounds, and he could piece them together to fool the lock.

"Just a few more. Try to fit bench, moon, trigger, and warrant into your answers. That will give her everything."

"That should be easy," Wizard said drolly.

"Not fucking helping," I muttered.

Ash managed to get in a couple of those words, then found others that would give her the final sounds she needed.

I sighed. "Got it. Give me five minutes."

After making a quick call, I began cleaning up the equipment we'd brought to the suite so we could tap into the surveillance at the hotel where the fundraiser was being hosted.

"Elias Prescott?"

I glanced at the monitor to see one of the waitstaff standing in front of Ash, wringing his hands and giving him a sympathetic frown.

"Yes?"

"Sir. I'm...I'm so sorry to have to tell you. The hospital just called. Your father...he collapsed, and they're rushing him into surgery. Your mom is asking for you."

Ash's brow slammed down, and he quickly handed Cynthia her bag before digging his phone out of his pocket. "Dammit. I turned it off."

He looked at Cynthia, who was wearing a mask of horror and sympathy.

"Darlin', I—"

"No! No!" she said with an understanding smile. "Go. I'll be absolutely fine. Go be with your mother."

"I—" He shook his head. Then he squeezed her hand and whispered, "Thank you."

Wizard started a slow clap as Ash rushed out of the ballroom.

I rolled my eyes. "I'd be gone when he gets here if I were you."

He grinned and continued helping me pack up.

"My dad in the hospital?" Ash scoffed as he stormed into the room, yanking off his bow tie. "You couldn't have come up with anything better? Do you know how fucking hard it was to pretend I cared?"

I shrugged. "Best I could think of to get you out fast while making sure she knew you wouldn't be home tonight. In an hour, send her a text to check in and let her know you'll be there for at least twenty-four hours."

"And if she calls the hospital?" he asked, narrowing his eyes at me.

"What? You think we're new at this shit?"

Ash deflated. "Right."

We'd set up a "private hospital" where Cynthia would be able to call and check on his dad's condition. There was even an address in case she decided to take it that far. It was guarded by a couple of our enforcers, dogs, and an electric fence. *For the privacy of the patients, of course.*

Ash's dad was actually on a ship with some donors who'd lost power and communication for the moment. It would probably be repaired by morning... assuming things went as we expected tonight.

Ash stripped out of the tux and pulled on a pair of jeans and a T-shirt. Then he turned to Wizard with a scathing expression. "You and I need to have a talk, brother? Because if I didn't know better, I'd think you were trying to get your ass handed to you."

"He's just trying not to think about the woman who won't give him the time of day," I answered.

"You don't know what the fuck you're talking about," Wizard groused as he closed up the last case and put it on the trolley we used to cart it up from our van.

"Violet and I have no secrets. You think she doesn't know what's going on with you and Thea?"

"We're not talking about this," he barked before slamming open the door and pushing the cart through it.

"Touchy," Ash joked.

"Talk to me when you're dealing with your own stubborn woman," I replied.

He scoffed. "Not gonna happen." He pointed at the tux balled up on the floor. "You, King, and Blaze got fucking lucky. Probably have the only three sane women in the world."

I laughed and tossed him his cut from the bed. "We'll see."

An hour later, we were staking out Ash's "house" —or the house we rented to solidify the illusion of Elias Prescott III—when King sent me a text to let me know that Cynthia had called to find out Ash's dad's condition.

Ten minutes later, Ash's phone buzzed with a security alert. "She's in the house."

He watched the feed on his phone for a few minutes, then glanced at me. "Make the call."

Wizard slid the door to the van open, and after I made an emergency call to 911, we all hopped out and crept toward the house.

Ash's server room was on the main level at the back of the house. Since Cynthia had shut off the security system, we were able to enter through the back door unnoticed.

We waited around the corner until we heard the voice key and Cynthia's wicked laughter before the heavy metal door squeaked as she pushed it open.

I glanced at my watch and murmured, "Five minutes out."

It would only take Cynthia a maximum of two minutes to get into the server and initiate the transfer of all of Ash's money to her accounts. We'd put an electronic trace on the funds so it left a trail everywhere it went, leading us to every nook and cranny of her finances.

Ace, King, and I had discussed simply making her destitute and ruining her name, but in the end, we wanted assurances that she wouldn't find another way to recreate her empire. Which was why we were allowing her to wire the money out before the cops arrived to take her in. At first, it would be for breaking and entering, then they'd discover the wire fraud, and finally, all the money she'd stolen.

We were there to make sure she didn't somehow get out before the police arrived.

When the sirens were close enough to be heard, the noise in the computer room ceased. The blaring horns grew louder, and she cursed.

The three of us quickly stepped up to the door to block her exit but were taken by surprise when she pulled a gun. Her maniacal gaze landed on Ash, and she screamed in outrage before pulling the trigger.

"Son of a bitch!" he roared as he staggered backward.

I was on her opposite side, so I shot out my hand to immobilize her wrist while Wizard snatched the gun and flipped the safety on.

"Ash?" I called.

"The safety was off?" Cynthia yelled, drowning out any response he might have given. Her voice was shaking with panic. "Oh fuck. Did I kill him? Shit!" Then she began to struggle like a lunatic—which didn't seem that far off at this point—and screaming, "Let me go! I'll kill you! Let me go, you bastards!"

"Ash!" I shouted again.

"Yeah, yeah. Just a fucking nick."

A relieved breath whooshed from my lungs, but I was stopped from being able to fill them again when Cynthia's elbow landed hard on my sternum.

"Wiz..." I gasped as pain knifed through my chest. "Take...can't...oh, fuck." Black spots danced before my eyes, and the pain became unbearable when I tried unsuccessfully to take in some air. Then everything went dark.

I blinked and batted at the bright light shining directly into my eyes. "Shit! Stop shining that thing before I go blind," I rasped. I sucked air into my lungs, relieved that it went in unobstructed.

"You fainted, man," Ash said before bursting into laughter.

I heard a female sigh. "He didn't faint, you butthead. His brain shut off from a lack of oxygen. There's a difference."

"Not when I tell the story," he choked out through his chortling.

"Sir?" the woman said more quietly. "Can you sit up and open your eyes? I just want to make sure you don't have a concussion from the fall."

I blinked again and winced at the brightness, but at least there was no flashlight shining right in my eyeballs.

Spoke too soon, I thought, when the EMT checked my pupils.

"Doesn't look like a concussion. That was a hard hit you took to the chest. How's your breathing?"

I nodded. "I'm sore, but nothing seems to be obstructing my flow of oxygen."

"Good," she replied with a smile. "I'd prefer to take you to the hospital to be checked out and just make sure she didn't crack your sternum. But..." She glared at someone off to the side. "With how freaking stubborn your friend is after being *shot*, I'm guessing a little pain in the chest is nothing compared to dealing with that...pain in the butt."

I chuckled and nodded. "You're right on all accounts..."

"Oh, my name is Nora," she told me with another smile. I took another good look at her and was surprised to see that she was very young. Probably no older than eighteen.

"Well, Nora. You're doubly right. Ash is a pain in the ass, and it's unlikely you'll talk me into going to the hospital."

She sighed and shook her head.

"I promise to get checked out, though, okay?" I offered.

Ash and I would both be looked over by Razor or Flint, doctors who were patched members. But I wouldn't be telling Nora about that.

She crooked up one corner of her mouth and gave me a small wave. "I'm going to give you the benefit of the doubt and believe you. It will help me sleep better at night."

I laughed and turned away, only to see Ash glaring at me.

"What?"

"Nothing," he said through gritted teeth.

Nora started to walk past him, and I watched in surprise when he gently grabbed her arm to stop her. "Only one you should be dreaming about tonight is me, baby girl."

She stiffened and raised her chin to a stubborn angle. "Dream on," she snapped.

"Oh, I will," he murmured before releasing her.

He watched her walk away with a myriad of emotions playing out on his face. It was clear he felt something for her but was confused and wary of it. If I had to guess, I'd say it was because of their age difference. There were probably twelve to fifteen years between them.

But that was his problem to deal with for now.

I needed to get back to my girl.

Unfortunately, giving witness statements, explaining the con, and making sure the right people were alerted so that Jean would be investigated for everything took a fuck ton of time. We didn't roll back up to the clubhouse until nearly nine in the morning.

Violet was standing with the girls in the lounge when I walked in. The second she saw me, she gasped and ran straight into my arms.

I captured her mouth in a long, drugging kiss before touching our foreheads together. "Fuck, I missed you."

"So...um, it's all done now?"

"Yep. Police are rounding up Jean's 'employees' now, and they received an anonymous packet this morning with the names and details of every victim we uncovered."

"That's...that's so great," she said with a smile that didn't reach her eyes.

What the hell was going on?

12

VIOLET

I had mixed feelings about the Hounds successfully taking down the con ring that Jeff was a part of. Obviously, I was happy for the people they'd taken advantage of because they'd get some form of repayment for the money they had lost. And that they couldn't hurt anyone else.

But I was worried about what it meant for Brodie and me.

He had no reason to stay in my apartment now that everything was wrapped up.

Showing yet again just how in tune he was to my feelings, Brodie asked, "What's wrong, baby?"

"I just...I kind of got used to having you live with me," I mumbled, feeling a little silly that I was complaining about not living together when our relationship was so new. It wasn't as though we still wouldn't be able to see each other as often as we wanted, but it just wasn't the same.

"And?" he drawled with a deep chuckle.

"I like sharing space with you." I twined my arms around his neck and smiled up at him. "Starting my morning cuddled with you in bed and ending it doing even better things in the same place. I really don't want to lose that."

"Who said you're gonna lose anything, baby? I thought we already went over this when we figured out who the head of the ring was." Gripping my hips, he tugged me flush against his chest. "Do you really think I'm gonna let you get away from me after I claimed you as mine?"

"No?" I whispered, butterflies swirling in my belly.

"You can say that with a fuck of a lot more confidence because I'm not going anywhere," he promised. "Not until we find a place to call our own, and then you'll be coming with me."

My lips curved into a grin. "Are you trying to tell me that my apartment isn't big enough for the two of us? I thought we've been quite comfortable since you moved in as my fake boyfriend."

"You know not a damn thing about our relationship is fake," he growled, grinding his hard-on against my stomach. "I might've jumped the gun by claiming that you were mine before we officially met, but I still meant it. From the very start, I knew that you belonged to me."

I toyed with the ends of his dark red hair at the back of his head. "It never hurts to double-check."

"Anytime you want me to demonstrate exactly how much you belong to me, just let me know." He trailed his lips down my jaw. "It'll be my pleasure. And yours."

"I will definitely take you up on that offer when we're somewhere a little more private." I glanced at Stella and King, and my lips curled down at the edges.

"What's wrong now, baby?"

"I'm not sure what the etiquette is here, if I'm supposed to ask or just wait and see..." I was having a hard time finding the right words to explain what I wanted.

"You never need to be shy with me, Violet." He tugged me over to the couch, dropping onto a cushion and pulling me onto his lap. "If there's something you need, I'm gonna figure out a way to give it to you. Doesn't matter what it is."

I took a deep breath while I gathered my courage. Then I blurted, "Am I really yours if I'm not wearing your property patch?"

"Is that what's bothering you, baby?" A wide grin stretched across his face before he put two fingers between his lips and whistled. When everyone turned to look at us, he called, "Hey, Prez! Did that order finally come in?"

"Yup, while you guys were out, as a matter of fact." King turned toward the prospect who was manning the bar. "There's a brown paper bag back there. Grab it for me."

"Sure thing, Prez."

The guy bent down to look under the bar and popped back up with the bag in his hand. Then he tossed it to King, who strode over to us. Brodie snagged the bag from him and reached inside to pull out a black leather vest that was sized for me.

Property of Echo was embroidered on a patch, and I traced the letters with trembling fingers. "You were already planning to claim me as your old lady?"

"Soon as this came in," he confirmed with a nod, gently lifting my arm to tug it through one of the holes in the vest. After he settled the leather against my back, he did the same with the other side. Then he gripped the lapels to pull me close. "Fuck, you look good with my name on you. Proclaiming to the world that you belong to me."

"I do, huh?" I twirled around in a circle, the breath catching in my throat at the possessive gleam in his eyes when I faced him again.

"Abso-fucking-lutely." He tilted his head to the side. "But something is missing."

My brows drew together as I glanced down at myself. "There is? What?"

"This."

I looked up and found him down on one knee in front of me, holding up a ring. The diamond solitaire twinkled in the light.

I could barely believe what I was seeing. Although his president and VP were both married, I hadn't expected him to propose quite so soon since we'd only known each other for about a month. But now that I truly thought about it, the same logic would've applied to him giving me his property patch, and that hadn't surprised me at all.

"You gonna answer me, baby? Or are you just gonna stand there lookin' like I just shocked the shit outta you so much that you can't even use that beautiful voice of yours?"

Ace leaned toward him and muttered, "Not sure that's how to get the girl to accept your proposal."

"Was it a proposal? Because I don't remember hearing him ask me to marry him," I teased.

"Shit," Brodie groaned, raking his fingers through his hair before getting to his feet and shoving the ring on my finger. "As long as I already fucked this up, I might as well just tell you that you're gonna marry me instead of giving you the chance to turn me down."

His response was so Brodie that I just giggled and went along with it. "Well, if you put it that way, I guess we're getting married."

"Soon, baby," he insisted, his lips brushing against mine as he whispered into my mouth. "Because I love you too damn much to wait to make you my wife."

"You love me?" I gasped, tears welling in my eyes over hearing those three little words from him.

"Of course, I do, baby." He shook his head with a deep laugh. "Fuck, I never actually said it before now, did I? It's a good thing I'm only ever going to propose once in my life because I'm no damn good at it."

"You're wrong. That was perfect," I disagreed,

shaking my head. "I love you too, Brodie. And I want nothing more than to be your wife. Except maybe to have your babies, too."

He patted my belly with a smirk. "Don't worry, baby. I'm doing my best to make sure that happens soon, too."

EPILOGUE
ECHO

"So?" I asked Violet as she stared out the front window of the house we were touring. "What do you think?"

"I—" She stopped abruptly and slapped her hand over her mouth as she spun around and darted out of the living room.

"Baby?" I called out with worry as I hurried after her. Seconds later, I found her by following the sounds of her retching. "Shit," I grunted, gathering her hair up so she didn't vomit in it.

She heaved a few more times, then plopped down onto her ass, exhausted.

"If you didn't like the house, you could have just told me," I teased as I grabbed a cloth I found under the sink and ran it under cool water.

A sigh fell from her lips when I set the dampened material on her forehead, then she chuckled. "Trust me, that wouldn't have been the way I'd told you."

"Yet you chose this method to tell me something else?" I asked as I hunkered down in front of her.

Violet frowned and tipped her head back to look up at me. "You think I'm trying to say something by throwing up?"

I grinned and shook my head. "Guess it was your body trying to get both our attention."

"Pardon?"

Cupping her face, I smiled softly and whispered, "Think we're havin' a baby."

Violet's eyes widened, and her face lit up like I'd just handed her the sun. "I'm pregnant?" she squealed. She bounced a little, then her face turned green, and she twisted around just in time to lose her stomach again.

"Come on, baby," I said quietly when she appeared to be done and some of the color was returning to her face. "Let's get you home. Then I'll run out and grab a test."

There were so many to choose from that I ended up grabbing five.

But I was glad I did when we were looking down

at all of the sticks lined up on the bathroom counter, all confirming that I'd knocked up my woman.

"I love you so fucking much," I murmured as I slipped my arms around her waist and rested my chin on her shoulder.

My hands cupped on her belly, and she set hers on top of them. "Love you, too."

After a few minutes of just standing there, reveling in the perfection of the moment, she turned around and wrapped her arms around my neck.

"Did you like that last house?" she asked, curiously.

"Yeah, but I'll like any house you love."

She smiled, and her eyes twinkled. "Are you sure it wasn't too isolated? It sits on over two acres."

"The farther away people are, the louder I get to make you scream," I muttered, grabbing her ass and boosting her up so she locked her legs around my waist.

"I already love it," she told me with a smirk, "but now I'm sold."

Laughing, I tossed her—more gently than usual since she was carrying my baby—and began undressing her. "How about we practice? I'll keep my hand over your mouth, and you show me just how loud you can be when I fuck you?"

Violet's eyes darkened to nearly black, and she shivered while her hands frantically worked my belt buckle. "Sounds extremely appealing," she said breathlessly.

Apparently, practice didn't make perfect, though. Once we were all moved in, she screamed my name so loud my ears were ringing. Now, our life was perfect.

EPILOGUE
VIOLET

Brodie had done as he promised, giving me the family I wanted. And it turned out that I carried the recessive gene for red hair, thanks to my great-great-grandmother. Because of her, we had a fifty-fifty chance of having the red-haired babies I wished for in my early days with Brodie. And we beat those odds since two of our three children were gingers like their daddy.

The youngest, our only daughter, had the temperament to go with her hair color, too. She also had her daddy and big brothers wrapped around her little finger, so I was the only one willing to put my foot down with her.

"Sorry, sweet pea. I already said no more cookies

tonight. You can have some apple slices instead, though, if you're still hungry."

Poppy puffed out her bottom lip in an exaggerated pout, widening her blue eyes for added effect. "No more cookies?"

"Nope." I shook my head. "Which you already knew because I told you the last one was it for the night."

"But Mom, she's only four. She doesn't understand," Brian defended his sister.

I quirked a brow at our eldest, who apparently needed to spend less time with his Uncle Ash because he enjoyed arguing a little too much and tended to blame it on the fact that he wanted to be a lawyer just like the club's secretary when he grew up. "How did your father and I teach you that there are consequences to your actions?"

My eight-year-old huffed out an irritated breath. "By enforcing the rules."

"And did we do the same with Brendan?"

Brian nodded, his shoulder slumping.

"So why should I treat your sister any differently?" I asked.

He pointed at Poppy. "Just look at her."

Big tears welled in her pretty eyes, and her hands

were pressed together in a pleading gesture. "Just one more. Pwease, Mommy?"

"Fine." I got up and stalked over to the plate of chocolate chip cookies that I'd baked earlier today, choosing the smallest one to give to her. "Here you go."

"Twank you, Mommy," she mumbled around the cookie she'd already shoved into her mouth.

"You caved?" Brodie asked, jerking his chin at our daughter as he walked back into the kitchen from the garage with Brendan right behind him. The boys took turns helping their dad take out the garbage each week, and he'd been up in the rotation.

"As if you would've been able to withstand the pressure," I scoffed, shaking my head. "You wouldn't have even tried to say no the first time around, and she probably would have talked you into a half a dozen more cookies, then woke us up in the middle of the night because she was sick to her stomach."

He couldn't argue because that had actually happened a few months ago. Instead, he turned to the kids and announced, "Time to get ready for bed."

Satisfied now that she'd gotten an extra extra cookie, Poppy climbed off her chair to race out of the kitchen. The boys looked as though they were going to argue for extra time, like usual, but one look at their dad's face, and they decided against it.

When they were gone, I leaned back in my chair, stretching out my legs before crossing my ankles. "You do realize that the day will come when the tables are turned, and you're the one feeling my pain while I take Poppy's side, right?"

"What do you mean?" Brodie asked, his brows drawing together.

I flashed him a mischievous grin. "When she's a teenager, she's going to want to go on dates. And you'll want to tell her that she can't...not until she's thirty, or something ridiculous like that, considering I was only twenty when we met."

"Damn straight, I'm not gonna let my baby girl date until she's way older than a teenager," he grumbled, crossing his arms over his broad chest.

"That's what you say now," I chirped with a shrug. "But how do you think she'll react to hearing her sweet daddy put his foot down for the first time in her life? While her teenage hormones are raging, and she has a crush on some boy..."

I trailed off, letting his imagination fill in the blanks.

"Fuck," he groaned, scrubbing his palms against his face.

I leaned forward to pat his leg. "I know it's hard to withstand those big, blue eyes, especially when they're aimed right at you with tears welling in them, and she pulls out that voice of hers. But you need to man up and act like the badass you really are, even if it makes her cry sometimes. Once she learns that you're going to make her follow the rules too, she might actually stop the fake tears."

"Maybe," he conceded with a deep sigh, shaking his head. "But she'll probably just come up with some other way to try to manipulate us into doing what she wants. And the odds are good it'll work. She might look like a mini female version of me, but she has your voice and brains. She's wicked smart for a four-year-old."

"Which is why we need to provide a united front. It's the only way we'll ever defeat her...I mean, successfully parent her."

Want to find out why Wizard knows so much about the romance author, Thea? Find out in Wizard!

In the mood for another pierced hero, but this time a little farther down his body? Check out I'm Yours, Baby!

And if you join our newsletter, you'll get an email from us with a link to claim a FREE copy of The Virgin's Guardian, which was banned on Amazon.

ABOUT THE AUTHOR

The writing duo of Elle Christensen and Rochelle Paige team up under the Fiona Davenport pen name to bring you sexy, insta-love stories filled with alpha males. If you want a quick & dirty read with a guaranteed happily ever after, then give Fiona Davenport a try!

Printed in Great Britain
by Amazon